BOUND BY THEIR NINE-MONTH SCANDAL

BOUND BY THEIR NINE-MONTH SCANDAL

DANI COLLINS

MILLS & BOON

First published in Great Britain 2019
by Mills & Boon, an imprint of HarperCollins*Publishers*
1 London Bridge Street, London, SE1 9GF

Large Print edition 2020

© 2019 Dani Collins

ISBN: 978-0-263-08428-3

MIX
Paper from
responsible sources
FSC
www.fsc.org
FSC® C007454

This book is produced from independently certified FSC™ paper to ensure responsible forest management. For more information visit www.harpercollins.co.uk/green.

Printed and bound in Great Britain
by CPI Group (UK) Ltd, Croydon, CR0 4YY

For my wonderful readers.
You make this possible. Thank you!

CHAPTER ONE

PIA MONTERO FEARED her sister-in-law's masquerade ball would be interminable, and it was, but not for the reason she had anticipated.

The October evening was cool, but dry. Guests had embraced the chance to cast off tuxedos and backless couture for something more exciting. Women twirled in overblown gowns with bell skirts, elaborate wigs and feathered headdresses. Men stalked in colorful brocade jackets with epaulettes and lace cuffs and short pants with stockings. Some even wore the *traje de luces* of a bullfighter with horned masks.

The masks were works of art. A few had cat ears and bird beaks, some covered an entire face, others were part of a jester hat with bells dangling from the cockscomb. Some were made from handblown Venetian glass, others were made of lace or satin and adorned with feathers and flowers, beads and sequins.

There were prizes for best costumes, but Pia had chosen to forfeit. She wore an understated gown in indigo topped with a purple velvet jacket. Her mask was a conservative cat's eye in molded silk painted with musical notes and roses, ideal for blending in.

She wished now that she'd chosen a full face mask as she watched a gold-lipped cherry blossom porcelain canvas swirl by. It would have allowed her to hide her thoughts behind a physical mask, rather than having to maintain the aloof expression she had practiced in the mirror at boarding school, back when she'd been hiding hurt feelings over *everything*, most especially being noticed.

Even when girls had stuck up for her back then, saying, "She's shy. Leave her alone," Pia had blushed and burned behind her breastbone, wishing herself into a hole in the ground because someone had looked at her.

Misery did not love company, as it turned out. She'd been lonely her entire childhood, too awkward to make friends and ridiculously smart, which had made her an academic rival, bookish and superior on top of all the rest.

Her saving grace was her bloodline. She came from Spain's aristocracy. Her parents were the Duque and Duquessa of Castellon, her father an innovator in industrial metals who had become a well-respected, elected member of parliament once his sons were old enough to take the reins on what was now a multinational corporation.

Pia was also reasonably attractive—not that she played it up. She eschewed makeup and designer wear, seeing little point in trying to attract a boyfriend when her mother would ultimately assign her a husband.

Which La Reina Montero was trying to do right now, turning a perfectly tolerable evening into something Pia struggled to bear.

"I'd prefer to wait until January, after I've defended my dissertation," Pia said, and braced herself, but it still stung when she received the expected *tsk* of tested tolerance.

Pia's brothers were chemical engineers, both unmarried until they were thirty, but Pia's accelerated study pace and soon-to-be-achieved doctorate only "wasted her best years," according to her mother.

"These things take time," her mother insisted. "Signal your interest. Was that the Estrada heir?"

Please no. Sebastián was decent enough, but he talked nonstop.

"His outgoing nature would balance your introversion. You'll have to work on that so you can host galas like this."

Say it louder, Mother.

"Perhaps if we go into the marquee, we can match names to the silent auction bids." La Reina tilted away her mask, which was mounted on a stick like a lorgnette. "I shouldn't have agreed to anything so childish as a masked ball. Very inconvenient."

"Most people seem to be enjoying themselves," Pia said mildly, noting laughter and noises of surprise as they approached the bustling tent where guests mingled while perusing the fund-raising items.

Ever the observer of animal behavior, especially human, Pia considered why a disguise would instill such high spirits. Was it the nostalgia of youthful play? She wouldn't know. Her childhood had been so rigid as to be a form of conditioned adulthood.

"Poppy is doing well." La Reina acknowledged her new daughter-in-law with reluctant approval as she glanced over the bids for rare vintage wines, antique jewelry, spa packages and VIP tickets to shows on Broadway and London's West End.

Did the masks reduce caution and provoke a willingness to take risks, Pia wondered? Similar to the way social media provided a removal from face-to-face interactions, thereby emboldening people to behave more freely?

Pia certainly felt at liberty to stare more openly. From behind the screen of her mask, she watched a couple debate a bid for a certain item. The woman protested it was too extravagant while the man insisted he loved her and wanted her to have it.

Pia was fascinated by interactions like that. They reminded her of the tenderness and indulgence that existed between her older brothers and their wives. They had both started their marriages in scandal, but had turned them into something meaningful, making her yearn for something like it for herself—as she repaired the family name by way of a low-drama, civilized marriage that was more a contracted merger with a dynasty of equal rank and prestige.

She bit back a sigh. Taking up the mantle of duty wasn't a sacrifice, she assured herself. It was a sensible course of action that benefited everyone, including herself. Her few attempts at dating had been failures, something the perfectionist in her loathed. Love and passion were foreign concepts. She wouldn't recognize either if she tripped over them.

She turned from spying on the couple and ran straight into a man setting down a pencil.

Physically the impact was light. With wistfulness blanketing her, however, the collision felt monumental. Life altering.

His opera cloak opened like dark wings that threatened to engulf her as his hands came up to grasp her upper arms and steady her.

Their masks had caused this, her confused mind quickly deduced. They interfered with peripheral vision. She wasn't clumsy or blind and doubted he was, either. He was too vital and controlled.

She recognized those traits in him instinctively, even though she wasn't usually sensitive to such things. Or sensual either, but she found herself taking in nonvisual elements even more swiftly than the sight of him. The heat of his body radiated around her. The strength in his hands was both gentle and firm. The scent of fresh air and orange blossoms clung to his clothing as though he'd arrived from a long walk through the grove, not from the stale air of a car.

Who was he?

His black tricorn hat had simple white trim. She glanced down to his black-on-black brocade vest over a black shirt, his snug black pants tucked into tall black boots.

A pirate, she thought, and looked back to his porcelain mask, white, blank and angular. It cast a shadow onto his stubbled jaw, his beard as black as the short hair beneath his hat.

She couldn't tell what color his eyes were,

but as he looked straight into hers, her pulse shot up with the race of a prey animal. She held that inscrutable stare, arms in his talon-like grip, skin too tight to contain the soar of emotion that rose in her.

Most people skipped past her in favor of more interesting folk, which she preferred. Sustained eye contact was never comfortable, but her mask gave her the confidence to stare back. To stare and stare while her whole body tingled in the most startling and intriguing way.

Sexual attraction? He possessed the attributes that typically drew female interest—height and broad shoulders, a firm physique and a strong jaw. She was stunned to learn she was human enough to react to those signals. In fact, as the seconds ticked by, the fluttering within her grew unbearable.

"Excuse me." Someone spoke behind her, jolting her from her spell.

A woman wanted to place a bid on Poppy's framed, black-and-white photo.

The black satin lining of the man's cloak disappeared as he dropped his hands from her arms. The noise around them rushed back, breaking her ears.

Pia moved out of the way. When she looked back, the man was leaving the tent.

Still trying to catch her breath, she moved to the bidding sheet where he'd left his pencil. She knew all the names on the list and none of those men had ever provoked a reaction like that in her.

At the bottom, in a bold scratch, was a promise to quadruple the final bid. It was signed *Anonymous*.

"How does this work?" Pia pointed to it as her mother finished speaking to someone and caught up to her. Pia's hand was trembling and she quickly tucked it into the folds of her skirt.

"It happens occasionally," her mother dismissed. "When a man wants to purchase something to surprise his wife."

Or didn't want his wife to know at all, Pia surmised. She wasn't a cynic by nature, but nor was she naive about the unsavory side of arranged marriages.

"He'll leave his details with the auctioneer," her mother continued. "It's a risky move that becomes expensive. Other guests will drive up the bid to punish him for securing the item for himself."

"The price one pays, I suppose." Pia's witticism was lost on La Reina.

"This is one of the paintings from the attic," La Reina said. "A modest artist. Deceased, which always helps with value, but not the sort of investment I would expect to inspire such a tactic."

Pia studied the portrait. The young woman's expression was somber. Light fell on the side of her round features, highlighting her youth and vulnerability.

"Do you know who she is?" Pia picked up the card.

"Hanging pictures of family is sentimental." Her mother plucked the card from her hand and set it back on its small easel. "Displaying strangers in your home is gauche."

"The final bid is sewn up," Pia pointed out. "I was merely curious."

"We have other priorities."

A husband. Right. Pia bit back a whimper.

* * *

Angelo Navarro nursed a drink as he clocked the rounds of the security detail, picking his moment for the second half of his mission.

He could have sent an agent to bid on the portrait, but along with not trusting anyone else with the task—loose lips and all that—the opportunity to slip onto the estate undetected had been far too tempting.

He hadn't expected such a bombardment of emotions as a result of visiting his birthplace, though. Anger and contempt gripped him; fury and injustice and a thirst for vengeance that burned arid and unquenchable in the pit of his belly.

These people prancing like circus clowns, making grand gestures with extravagant bids to benefit victims of violence, were the same ones who had ignored a young woman's agonizing situation. They hadn't interfered when her child had been taken from her and had continued to revere her persecutors.

Angelo felt no compunction whatsoever at infiltrating this private fund-raiser with the intention of retrieving what his mother had stolen. Or been given. He'd never been clear on how she had obtained the jewelry or exactly which pieces had gone missing. That part didn't matter. He would happily have gone to his grave with the knowledge that she'd fought back in her own way.

However, when this chance to add a fresh blow had arisen, he hadn't been able to resist it.

Did it make him as soulless as his father that he was willing to commit a criminal act to continue her retaliation? So he could show his half brothers how it felt to be toyed with and abandoned to poverty?

Perhaps.

The thought didn't stop him. He casually made his way to the corner of the house, waited for the guard's attention to turn and slipped into the dark beyond.

He came up against a Family Only sign on the first step of the spiral staircase and smirked with irony as he slipped past it to climb to the rooftop patio.

The stairs gave a nostalgically familiar creak

as he reached the top—where he discovered someone had arrived ahead of him.

The sound and light from the party were blocked by the rise of the west wing of the house, casting the space into deep shadow. He could only see a silhouette and the lighter shadow of her mask as she turned from gazing across the moonlit Mediterranean. Even so, he recognized her as the woman who had careened into him as he was bidding on the portrait of his mother.

For one second as he'd steadied her, he had forgotten everything—his thirst to punish, his purpose in coming here. Something in her uninspired costume gave him the impression she didn't belong here any more than he did. That she was hiding in plain sight. His male interest had been so piqued, he had nearly asked her to dance.

"Oh." The lilt in her voice told him she had identified him from their brief encounter as well, which also told him she had found it as profound as he had.

"Were you expecting someone else?" He adjusted his mask to peer harder into the shadows. The rickety bench where his mother used to read to him was gone, replaced by a dark shape that suggested a comfortable, L-shaped sectional.

"I wasn't expecting anyone."

That was good news. On many levels.

"Did you follow me?" she asked.

"No." He would like to think he would have timed things differently if he had known she was up here, but he wasn't sure. Nor was he as dismayed as he ought to have been that she was now an obstacle to his goal.

"Did *you* invite someone to join you?" she asked, vaguely appalled.

He should have said, *Yes*. She sounded so uncomfortable at intruding, she probably would have hurried away, but something in him balked at letting her think he was involved with anyone.

He heard himself say a throaty and inviting, "Not yet."

Her silhouette grew more alert. The air crackled between them.

"Who are you?" Her voice sharpened and her mask tilted as she cocked her head.

It struck him that he couldn't tell her. *Damn.*

"I think the purpose of a night like this is to maintain the mystery."

"And telling me would identify you as the buyer of that portrait you bid on so generously. And anonymously."

"True." The peril he was in began to impact him. She could place him with the painting and here on the rooftop. Maybe she didn't know his name, but there was a chance she could find out.

Dared he linger? Was it worth the risk?

He couldn't tell whether this rooftop patio had been repaved or the old bricks merely pulled up and reset, exposing the hidey-hole he had discovered as a child. He doubted his half brothers had ever found it. If they had, they wouldn't have been so sly in their sale of this estate. There was every chance the new owners had found the treasure, though, and kept the contents without mentioning it. Angelo had very little faith in humanity, particularly those who sat like cream on the top of society without having worked to get there.

He couldn't leave until he knew for sure.

He had come this far, and so decided to wait her out.

He joined her at the wall. The last time he'd been here, he'd barely been tall enough to peer over. His distant memory of that time was swept away by the breeze off the water and the woman's voice beside him.

"If you didn't follow me or come to meet someone, why are you here?"

"Curiosity." It wasn't a complete lie. He was definitely intrigued by her. "You?"

"To think."

"About?"

"The nature of happiness. Whether it's a goal worth pursuing when there are no guarantees I'll find it. That it would come at the expense of others if I did."

"Nothing too heavy, then," he drawled. Her hand was close to his on the wall, pale and ringless. "In my experience, happiness is a fleeting thing. A moment. Not a state of being."

"And if a moment is all you have?"

His scalp prickled beneath his hat. He turned his head and tucked his chin, trying to see through the dark and the holes in his mask to read her expression, but it was impossible.

"Regret is also a moment. A choice *not* to seize happiness when it presents itself."

"I *would* regret it if I didn't take a chance," she agreed with a nod of contemplation.

"What kind of chance?"

She let a couple of seconds tick by with crushing silence, then said in a thicker voice, "An overture. Letting my interest in someone be known." Her hand had been curled into a tense fist, but it unfurled, her pinkie finger splaying toward him.

His stomach knotted. "Are you married?"

"No." Through the rush of relief in his ears, he heard her add, "But obligations to do so loom. And I don't want to risk making a fool of myself when I don't know if he's even—"

"He is," he cut in. His chest felt tight and his throat could barely form words. "He's interested."

CHAPTER TWO

PIA'S HEART WAS pounding so hard, she ought to have hammered down the walls around her.

"Do you know who *I* am?" she asked faintly.

"Should I?"

"No." If he did, he would be treating her differently. With kid gloves, because of her family's influence. There would be no intimate questions about whether she was meeting someone or encouragement to act impulsively.

It was enormously refreshing not to carry the weight of history and expectation, which had been the nature of her dilemma when she'd come up here. That ever so brief moment with him in the marquee had sent her into a spiral of doubt about duty to family versus selfish pursuits.

"Are *you* married?" she asked.

"I'm not involved with anyone. But a moment is all I have, too." His velvety timbre was layered with regret.

She kept trying to place his voice, certain she would remember if she'd heard him before.

"I don't even know what I want except not to let this moment pass without..."

"Seizing it?" he suggested.

"Stealing it," she said wryly, finding the idea deeply seductive. It was the best of both worlds. She could briefly shed mousy, dutiful Pia Montero without giving her up for good. It was *safe*.

"Strangers in the night." He held out a hand as if inviting her to dance.

Her hand went into his even though the music was a distant drone without a discernible tempo.

He was too compelling to resist, though. It wasn't the outfit, either. She understood that some animals were innately dominant. He was one of them and he ought to send her scurrying, but she was too fascinated. She was utterly riveted by him and her reaction to his air of supremacy.

She distantly noted that she would have to

tell her mother to find her a good-natured beta male so she wouldn't be so completely overwhelmed by the simple act of being held in a man's arms.

This was biology, she told herself through the fog of her deepening attraction. She was reacting to a chemistry that didn't come from a mix of beakers, but from the scent of pheromones off skin. Receptive male meets receptive female. The pseudoerotic nature of their disguised identities and their clandestine meeting on an unlit rooftop exaggerated the excitement.

But even as her head tried to explain it and dismiss it, her body grew pliant and her feet shifted closer into his sphere. She wasn't acting like herself, but she would never have an encounter like this again, when she could *be* someone else, free of commitment and the constraints of being Pia Montero. When her physical appearance and other shackles of identity were so absent she was nothing but the energy of pure, universal womanhood.

And he was all man.

"I want to kiss you," he said in a voice that rumbled deep in his chest.

Her pulse skipped. It was only a kiss. She wanted to feel his mouth, to *experience* him. "I want that, too."

"Come here."

It was magnetic attraction rather than his arms that pulled her as she followed him into the shadow of the chimney. She couldn't discern his features at all as he slipped his mask up, knocking his hat away.

His arms encircled her and his mouth brushed against her cheek, seeking and finding hers.

An electric current jolted through her at first contact, leaving her tense and waiting when he drew back slightly, his breath catching the way hers had.

She wasn't great at kissing. It was yet another of those human interactions that had eluded her, but as his mouth returned, she discovered she liked it. His lips settled firmly across hers, flooding her with incredible heat, smooth and unhurried. As if they had all the time in the world for stolen kisses.

Her hand found his stubbled cheek and she enjoyed the abrasion against her palm as much as the lazy play of his mouth against hers. He teased her like that a few times, deepening the kiss with incremental degrees until she was parting her lips to catch his, wanting more. Her tongue darted out on instinct, practically begging for more.

With a growl in his throat, he settled into a hot kiss of intense passion, something she recognized with a fresh jolt of surprise and excitement. Then she lost the ability to consider what was happening to her as his strong arms pulled her into a world of pure sensual pleasure. The strength and safety of his embrace was all that held her together as she shuddered under an onslaught of pleasure so intense a helpless noise throbbed in her throat.

"Stop?" he whispered against her lips.

"Never. This is…" *Overwhelming. Glorious. Essential.*

She touched the back of his head, brought him back into the kiss and tried to give him the same sort of pleasure she was receiving. She offered all of herself, completely open to whatever he needed. She had never experienced anything so extraordinary.

He made another noise, this one more unfettered, as though he was slipping loose of whatever sort of control he held himself under—which perversely thrilled her. His hands stroked firmly through the layers of her velvet jacket and full skirt, molding her form, lighting a fire under her skin, sending a heavy ache into her loins.

"I've never felt like this," she told him in a rasp of need, burrowing her hands beneath his cloak, into the heat beneath his vest. She had never been so forward, seeking so compulsively to touch a man, to take in his textures and musculature.

He swore. "Me, either." His hand cupped the back of her neck and his breath pooled hotly against her throat. "But this can't happen." He scraped his teeth against her nape, making her nipples pinch into sharp sensitivity. "I can't start something. I was never here."

"Neither was I," she said with a choke of rusty laughter. "Keep going."

Her greedy hands went down to his butt.

She had never done such a thing, never realized that the hard flex of his glutes could offer such a thrill as she squeezed.

He did the same to her, his strength pulling her so close she felt the shape of his erection through his trousers and the velvet of her dress, hard against her belly. Her brain distantly processed his arousal as potentially alarming, but her body fairly melted under a hot flush of desire.

"Yes. Like that," she said in an agonized whisper. She had never been more thrilled by anything in her life.

He muttered something about wrong time and place, but he pressed her beneath him onto the lounger, his cloak falling heavily around them. He kissed across her bare collarbone, whiskers abrading her skin. When his hand sought beneath her, she arched so he could lower her zipper and loosen her bodice.

She was braless and he groaned with gratitude as he cupped her naked breast and lightly scoured her skin with his stubbled cheek before he closed his mouth over her nipple.

Desire was such a knifing ache in her that

she swallowed a cry and arched again, unable to get close enough. She struggled against the confines of her skirt, ground herself against the ridge of his erection, yearning for the pressure of him *there*. Between. Where she was damp, her pulse throbbing like a signal.

"This is insane." He lifted his head, looming like a gothic shadow over her, dangerous and fierce—but she wasn't terrified at all.

"It's a memory," she murmured. "A good one."

His breath cascaded across her cheek in a rasp of disbelief. Agreement. He caught her earlobe in his teeth, sending delicious shivers through her whole body.

When he lifted himself again to drag her skirt upward, she bent her knee to help, embracing the chilly air against her naked thigh, excited by the fabric of his trousers as he settled between her legs.

"I don't have anything."

"A condom?" She hadn't thought of that. This was the point when they ought to stop. *She knew that.*

"Are you on anything? I don't have any health issues."

She wasn't, but she had thrown supplies in her clutch this evening, thinking her cycle was due and didn't it always arrive at the least convenient time.

"I'm okay. It's fine." She didn't want to stop. There would never be another moment like this one. She needed him more than she needed air.

His hand cupped her cheek. "Thank you." It was the growl of an animal loosed from a cage and threatening to consume her. His busy mouth went across her jaw and down her throat and back to her breast while she ran her hands over and over the layers of clothing across his back.

When he stroked his broad hand up her thigh, she got her hands beneath his clothing, too; found the hot, smooth skin of his waist and the hollow of his spine. She would have tried to work her hand around to open his belt, but his thumb slid inward to graze over the silk between her legs.

She gasped and went very still.

"No?" He froze.

"Yes." She could barely speak, the yearning in her grew so sharp.

"Mmm…" He did it again and caught her light cries with his kiss, making love to her mouth with his tongue as he teased and caressed and his thumb found its way beneath silk to stroke into slippery heat.

She shuddered as she kissed him back, flagrant and uninhibited, playing her tongue against his, her hands roaming everywhere she could reach. She was trying to convey how much pleasure he was giving her. Trying to reciprocate it.

"You're gorgeous," he told her as he lifted himself just enough to unbuckle and release his fly.

"You can't see me." She searched the dark, trying to make out the shadowed features so close to her own, but there was only the black cutout of his silhouette against the blanket of stars above them.

"I see you." His eyes glittered despite the lack of light, making it seem as though he saw all the way into her soul. "Sensual. Curious. Pensive. And courageous enough to steal what you want." He kissed her with a smile on his lips.

"I'm not courageous at all— *Oh*."

He slid her panties to the side and settled his hot, hard, naked flesh against hers.

She throbbed with anticipation. *Ached*. She knew he was about to ruin her for whatever husband lay in her future, not because he would take her virginity, but because no man would ever make her feel this way again. Elemental and beautiful. *Free*.

"I see power." She let her fingers move through the short, silky strands of his hair, petting this dangerous wolf who could devour her, but held her in thrall instead. "Self-discipline and patience and intelligence."

"I'm none of those things. Not right now." His voice skimmed across her cheek while the crown of him, fierce and hot and hard searched against her damp, untried folds.

"You're perfect," she insisted.

The party was a distant soundtrack, her self-control long thrown away.

She had no regrets as she felt the press of him, the pinch and sting of his shape forging into her. She didn't even care if she orgasmed. She was thrilled enough by this—the act of finding a lover who pleased her. Of choosing him and by extension choosing herself. It was selfishness in the extreme and a moment of physical connection that would always be hers—something she would reach for to soothe the bleak isolation that would continue to be her constant companion through the rest of her life.

He nibbled at her jaw as he rocked his hips, settling himself fully inside her. "You feel incredible."

"You, too," she murmured, dazed by the intensity of lying with him this way. Clothed and joined, his weight crushing her lower half while his arms cradled her. His scent was a drug, his lips tender and teasing.

On instinct, she sought his mouth, perhaps looking for reassurance, but it turned passionate quickly. It was such a remarkable, glorious feeling to kiss like this while their bodies were locked. She wished they were naked. He was so gloriously, beautifully wonderful.

With a growl, he shifted, braced on an elbow

as he withdrew and returned in a slow, testing stroke.

The friction caused an acute stab of pleasure that left ripples of shivery sensations in its wake. She gasped and dug her fingernails into his shoulders, astonished.

He chuckled softly. Roughly.

"That was something, wasn't it? Perhaps we're being spared by the gods. If I had met you any other time, I would chain you to my bed forever," he threatened.

If only...

He moved again, making all of her sing. She clutched at him, trying to make sense of the sensations overtaking her, but it was far too engulfing. She found it impossible to think, only feel. There was a sting and heat and a kind of tension she had never experienced. She wanted to absorb herself into his skin, but there were so many barriers. All she could do was hang on as he cast off restraint and moved with more purpose. Their breaths grew more jagged, each stroke making her fight cries of increasing pleasure.

She didn't know how to communicate to him

how dazzling and wonderful this was except to allow animal instinct to overtake her. She licked his throat and offered her hips for the driving force of his. She stroked her hands beneath his shirt against his lower back, encouraging his rough possession while she brazenly sucked at his bottom lip.

And just when she thought she couldn't rise one more degree of arousal, couldn't take one more second of this onslaught of sensation, nature took over again and her climax swept her up into the heavens above them.

He stiffened, tightened his grip on her and stopped breathing exactly as she did. Then he shuddered and ragged cries sounded against her neck while she opened her mouth in a silent scream, all of her world shattering around her, leaving her destroyed, never to be the same again.

Angelo touched a kiss to the top of her spine as he finished zipping her dress.

She let her hair fall and adjusted her mask as she turned to offer her mouth to his.

He took a final, lingering taste of her, trying to memorize the exact plump shape of her lips with the sweep of his tongue. When he drew back, he searched through the faint light cast by the party on the far side of the house, aware that he would spend the rest of his life looking for this pointed chin, that wide mouth and elegant forehead framed by this fall of dark hair.

Against his better judgment, he almost asked for her name, but she spoke first.

"We should get back." There was a creak of misery in her voice. She caught at his hand and pressed his knuckles to the hot pulse in her throat. "Thank you."

"Thank *you*."

It was an impossible situation. He wasn't supposed to be here. And much as he was enthralled by her sexually, he didn't know if he could trust her. It was best to leave this as a torrid, dream-like encounter.

"I'll go first and distract the guards. They won't be alarmed I've been up here."

"Because you're a woman?" Females could be treacherous. His grandmother had been one of the cruelest. But the guards might be tempted to frisk him if they caught him leaving a private area. He appreciated her giving him a clear path of escape.

"Until we meet again," he said as he adjusted his mask and hat.

"In another life," she said with a melancholy pang in her voice, turning away to begin her descent.

With one ear cocked for voices or a return of her footsteps, he moved into the corner of the patio. He flicked on his cell phone for light and noted that, aside from a thorough cleaning of the moss that took root every winter, the new owners had left the bricks exactly as he remembered them. He only had to move a planter of dormant flowers to expose the familiar, hexagonal brick beneath. He pried it up with the blade of his pocketknife and shone a light in to check for vermin or prevent a nasty spider bite.

The space was dry and empty—except for the tobacco tin. He drew it out and opened it long enough to see the glitter of jewels and the head of a small plastic wolf—one of his own treasures tucked away so his brothers wouldn't steal it, melt it, or otherwise use it to torment him.

In the distance, the music stopped. A male voice said something about costume judging.

With a well-practiced move, Angelo smoothly set the brick back into place. He slid the tin into the pocket of his cloak as he straightened.

Moments later, as he slipped down the stairs and past the sign that read Family Only, his brain quit replaying the most exquisite love-making of his life and made the connection.

The guards wouldn't be alarmed at her presence in a private area *because she was family.*

He swallowed an imprecation and waited to look at his phone until he had melted past the party perimeter and hiked through the orange grove to his car. It took two swipes to bring up a photo of the new owner of the estate, Rico Montero. Another swipe and there was Rico's sister, Pia.

Angelo knew that pillowy bottom lip. Intimately. He knew how her vanilla skin tasted. The silk of her hair against his brow still tickled him with sensual memory.

His lover wasn't a cast-off mistress of a playboy or a daughter of a businessman trying to elevate her circumstances. Her forlorn, *It's a memory. A good one* had made him think she lived some sort of deprived existence, but how rough could her life be?

He knew women could be in an abusive situation without it being apparent to the world, but Pia held a lot of aces. She earned dividends from the family corporation run by her brothers, lived in a small but elegant house in a very exclusive neighborhood. Her social media page was covered in photos of exotic landscapes.

She came from a family exactly like Angelo's father and brothers—titled and entitled. Angelo already knew the Montero brothers' scandalous affairs with vulnerable women, a PA and a housemaid, had been papered over with quickie marriages, the Duque's political career and the family's positions of power and wealth left unscathed.

As for Pia, her fine-boned features were even more patrician and elegant without the mask. She was photographed at the occasional gala, her smiles unapproachable, her poses as deliberately nonchalant as a fashion model showing off a runway gown.

That lissome figure had been delightfully supple. He experienced a latent pulse of heat recalling the feel of her writhing beneath him, but she wasn't his type. He preferred bubbly, outgoing women with real jobs. Ones whose motives and interest in him were crystal clear. He had learned the hard way that his wealth made him a target for the decidedly mercenary members of either sex.

He threw his phone onto the passenger seat and pulled away, disgusted with himself for giving in to impulse with someone so *wrong*.

It wasn't the snobbery of an upstart toward the bastion of old money or the petulance of being shut out of that privileged life and therefore wanting to tear it down. His contempt went far deeper. Someone must have known what had gone on in that cottage on the Gomez estate all those years ago, but they had chosen to ignore it. They had continued associating with monsters, enabling Angelo's father and brothers to enjoy a level of status they had no right to. His father should have been jailed and, when the old baron died, Angelo should have received a portion of his estate.

Despite being fourteen and away at boarding school, still grieving his mother's suicide, Angelo had been abandoned and turned onto the street. Angelo was convinced his brothers had deliberately burned down his mother's cottage, both for the insurance money and to prevent him returning to live there.

Angelo had scrambled to survive and if his brothers had left him to make his new life, he might have left them to living their old one. Instead, when they realized a cache of jewelry was missing, they had come after Angelo, accusing him and his mother of theft.

Given the way Angelo had been living, his brothers had believed him when he'd said he didn't have anything but the shirt on his back, but they had been convinced he knew where the jewelry was hidden.

As he proved tonight, Angelo had had a very good idea where his mother had buried the treasure, but no amount of being knocked around or intimidated had got that secret out of him. Instead, he had bit his split lip and resolved to destroy them, no matter how long it took.

Angelo could have come forward as the baron's bastard anytime in the last decade and a half, demanding his share of their father's estate through legal channels. Aside from having no desire to acknowledge that half of his DNA, it would have been expensive. Until the last few years, he hadn't been able to afford that sort of fight. It also would have turned his mother's anguish into nothing more than sordid muckraking in the press. He couldn't do that to her memory.

Besides, he had perversely enjoyed his brothers' fruitless search. If they had ever managed to unearth the jewels, he would have staked his claim. It was, after all, compensation his mother had taken with the knowledge she would never be left anything by Angelo's father beyond the use of a run-down cottage.

As far as Angelo was concerned, this tin of jewelry was his inheritance, fair and square.

He might have let his brothers go to their graves thinking the fortune well and truly lost if the masquerade ball hadn't presented such a perfect opportunity to collect it. If they hadn't sold the estate in such an underhanded deal and put his mother up for auction as if they were philanthropists for doing so...

They made him sick.

As he reached the field where his helicopter waited and climbed aboard with the weight of the tin in the pocket of his cloak, he considered when and how he would reveal to them that he did indeed possess what his mother had taken.

He wanted them in the weakest possible position, fully on the ropes, when he dealt this blow. Currently, they were still living off the proceeds of selling the estate to Rico Montero. Those funds would run out quickly, given Darius's gambling habits and Tomas's recent divorce. When they began to look hungry, Angelo would tip his hand.

It would drive them crazy. They would want to stake a claim, but doing so would force them to admit their family connection. They would have to admit how Angelo had come to exist and how his mother had got her hands on these diamonds and pearls.

Angelo would enjoy seeing them twist and turn against each other when that happened.

Like every nearly perfect caper, however, there was one witness who could blow the whole thing apart. Pia Montero.

She could place Angelo on the estate this evening.

If she discovered who he was.

CHAPTER THREE

Six weeks later...

"WOULD YOU EXCUSE me a moment?" Pia said to her mother and Sebastián.

She didn't wait for her mother's permission or even glance to read what was likely an expression of disapproval. Her mother probably thought she was giving in to nerves, but Pia didn't care. She rose abruptly from the table and hurried to the toilet, where she lost every bite of the lunch she'd just eaten.

What on earth?

She wrung out a cloth and dabbed the perspiration from her wan face, shocked at the violence of her sudden illness. She'd been feeling odd all week, thinking she might be coming down with something, but she wasn't running a fever. She wouldn't dare accuse her mother's chef of anything less than using the freshest ingredients.

That left one obvious explanation before she went down the road of blood panels for exotic diseases.

But it was impossible. Her cycle had arrived the day after the masquerade ball. That ought to mean she wasn't pregnant. However, she realized with another roll of her tender stomach, she hadn't had a period since.

She couldn't be pregnant. *Couldn't.* Her mother's top tier, preferred choice for Pia's husband was in the dining room *right now.*

Think, she commanded her rattled brain, but she was too shaken and confused to even recall the dates and count the weeks properly.

She would put off reacting until she'd had it confirmed, she resolved. And she would take a test immediately.

She fought her composure back into place and returned to the dining room, but didn't retake her seat.

"I'm very sorry, Mother. I'm not feeling well and have to go home. May I call you later in the week to try this again, Sebastián?"

"Let me drive you home." He rose and set aside his napkin.

"I wouldn't want to impose. Mother's driver collected me. I'll have him run me back."

"Not at all. Thank you for lunch, La Reina. I look forward to seeing you again soon."

Pia's mother offered a meaningless smile and tilted her cheek for his air-kiss, but her glance toward Pia warned that a lecture would be forthcoming.

Moments later, Pia was beside Sebastián in his sports car.

Through lunch they had established that they both enjoyed scuba diving and beachcombing. He mostly worked out of Madrid, but had holidayed as a child in Valencia and would love to settle in this area once he was raising a family. His mother bred show dogs and he had taken a runt out of pity. He admitted to shamelessly spoiling it, which had made her mother smile stiffly while Pia had experienced a weak ray of optimism. Perhaps they could have a successful marriage after all.

"I'm very sorry," she apologized again. "I've

been fighting something all week and should have canceled."

"In sickness and in health, right?" His bold calling out of today's less than subtle agenda made her stomach roil all over again. She couldn't lead him on if she was carrying another man's child.

"Sebastián, I think we should slow down."

He took his foot off the accelerator, instantly alert. "Oh, you mean—" He glanced at her, then made an abrupt turn into the parking lot of a mechanic's garage. "Did I say something to offend you?"

"Not at all. But something has come up that makes me think it's best if we put off discussions until the new year."

She tried for a polite smile and a poker face, but the longer he searched her expression, the more culpable she felt. She had to look away.

He cleared his throat, then spoke carefully. "It may surprise you to hear there are very few circumstances that would put me off what we're contemplating."

She licked her numb lips. "You don't realize how serious this circumstance might be."

"I think I do." He sounded so grave, so sure, she closed her eyes in dread.

Was it obvious? Would rumors circulate before she'd had a chance to confirm it? To discover the identity of the father and tell him?

For the first time since she was a child, her eyes grew hot and her throat swelled with the urge to cry.

"My family wants this alliance quite badly, Pia. I'm not without a checkered past that you would have to accept. Offering solutions and protection to one another is the point of this sort of partnership. Please talk to me about anything you view as an impediment to our moving forward. I'm quite sure I can accommodate you."

She wanted to goggle at him, unable to believe he would be willing to take on another man's child, but he reached across and squeezed her hand with reassurance.

She swallowed and found a faint smile. "Let me call you later in the week, after I've had time to think some things through."

"Of course."

He took her home, but she only stayed long

enough to double-check her dates and call her sister-in-law.

An hour later, she was halfway up the coast. She stopped at a village market and bought an off-the-shelf pregnancy test, took it into a service station restroom and sat in her car a long time afterward, absorbing the fact that she was carrying a baby.

The baby of a man she didn't know. At all.

She was a smart, responsible woman. How could she have been so careless?

She didn't let herself dwell on the fact that both her brothers had been through this. That maybe some dark and desperate part of her had sabotaged herself into this position, hoping to find a version of the happiness Cesar and Rico had both found.

That sort of thinking was beyond illogical. It was self-destructive.

And genuinely impossible when she didn't even know her lover's name.

But that was why she wanted to see Poppy.

She put her car in Drive and returned to the scene of the crime.

* * *

Half an hour of mutual admiration with her two-year-old niece restored a little of Pia's equilibrium.

Despite the circumstances, she looked forward to motherhood, she realized with a small bubble of optimism. She wouldn't be a distant, coldly practical woman like her mother, even though she already knew La Reina would judge her harshly for showing affection toward her child. She scolded Sorcha and Poppy for it often and Pia could still hear her mother rebuking her own nanny for hugging her.

Don't spoil her. She'll become dependent.

Yes, it must have been the early hugs, not the lack of them thereafter that had turned Pia into the withdrawn, insecure, social-phobic person that she was.

"Will you go with Nanny while I talk to your *mamà*?" Pia asked Lily.

Lily gave Pia's neck a fierce hug and said, "I yuv you," in English, bringing tears to Pia's eyes as the small girl waved bye-bye on her way out the door.

She would have that soon—someone who would say those words and mean it, every day.

"I think I got some good ones," Poppy said, setting aside her camera as they entered the lounge. "Thank you. I'm making an album for Rico for Christmas. I don't know what else to get the man who has everything."

Pia's brother Rico had been in a bad place after his brief first marriage had ended in tragedy. Then he had discovered that Poppy had had his daughter in secret. Since locating them, he'd become more like the brother Pia recollected from her earliest years, before he left for school; the one who was patient and protective, willing to sit with an arm around her so she felt safe as she watched an evil witch in a children's movie.

"Coffee? Wine?" Poppy offered.

Pia faltered as she realized she was off alcohol and likely coffee, as well. Good thing she had barely touched what her mother had served.

"I came from lunch at Mother's. Nothing for now, thank you."

"Did she say something about the auction?

Is that why you're here?" Poppy winced as she sat. "When you said you wanted to ask me about it, I thought you wanted the auctioneer's card." She picked it up from a side table. "Am I in trouble?"

"No. But I would like that, if you don't mind." Pia pocketed the card. "No, Mother is quite pleased you broke records on the fund-raising, even if she doesn't agree with your methods."

"Because of the painting," Poppy said heavily, shoulders slumping.

"I meant the costumes. Mother thinks that sort of thing is a gimmick. What are you talking about? Which painting?"

"The one from the attic. The young woman. She's the reason I raised so much. The bidder paid a ridiculous sum."

"I remember it. Who bought it?" She held her breath.

"That's the trouble. I don't *know*."

"The auctioneer didn't tell you?"

"Wouldn't," Poppy said flatly. "I *tried*. The previous owners were upset and wanted to know."

"Baron Gomez?"

"And his brother, yes. Do you know them?"

"Only vaguely by reputation." Not a good one. The family had fallen on hard times after the previous baron's death. One brother was a womanizer, the other a gambler. Neither was particularly adept at business. Both were too old to be her mystery man and too young to have fathered him. "Why were they upset?"

"Good question! They sold us the property as is, with all sorts of furniture and other items left behind. When I found the painting in the attic, I thought it was rather good so I called the family as a courtesy, to be sure they wouldn't mind my auctioning it for the fundraiser."

"Did they say who she was?"

"Their stepsister, the daughter of their father's second wife. She lived in a cottage at the corner of the property. It burned down after she died. She must have passed at a young age. She looks about fifteen in the portrait and it was painted thirty years ago. In any case, the new baron struck me as rather callous when he laughed and said, 'Sure, see what you can get for her.'"

"Was he at the ball?"

"They declined the invitation. But he asked me to note that he had donated the painting."

Pia wanted to roll her eyes at the man's "generosity," but was too well-bred.

"I should have told Rico that something felt off, but I thought I was being sensitive."

"Why? What happened?"

"The painting went for a hundred thousand euros! Someone quadrupled the final bid to ensure they would get it."

Pia hadn't known it had gone for *that* much. "What was the painting assessed at?"

"Five hundred euros."

"I see." She didn't. At all. But it was nice to know her baby's father had a generous streak.

"I *know*. I wanted to thank him personally, but the auctioneer said the purchaser specifically requested I send my thank-you to the Gomez family for donating it and that I should tell them how much I got for it. Your mother said it was crass to mention the figure, but that since it was such a substantial donation I should honor his wishes." Poppy's eyes went wide again. "Huge mistake."

"Why?"

"For starters, I don't think the Gomez family would have let me sell it if they'd realized I would get that sort of money for it. First the younger one, Darius, called me and went *crazy*. He was swearing and making threats, trying to get me to tell him who bought the painting. He wouldn't believe I didn't know. I was upset and told Rico. He called the older one and tore *such* a strip off him. My Spanish vocabulary was deeply enriched, let me tell you." Poppy was making light of it, but Pia could tell she was still unsettled.

"I wonder if the purchaser knew what kind of hornet's nest he was stirring up," Pia said, even though she instinctively knew he must have. The man she'd met had seemed extremely sure of himself.

"I'm quite sure I was pushed into the middle of a battlefield. When Rico hung up, he asked if someone named Angelo Navarro had been on the guest list. I guess that was the name of the person the Gomez brothers suspected was behind the purchase. I checked and he wasn't on it, but anyone could have placed that bid on his behalf."

I was never here.

A cold prickle left all the hairs on Pia's body standing on end.

"Angelo Navarro," she murmured. "Do you know who he is?"

"Rico did some research. He's a tech billionaire who came up *very* recently. Quite predatory. He's targeting the Gomez interests… 'Picking off the low-hanging fruit,' Rico said. Rico told your mother's assistant to bar all of them from any future events. I didn't realize there was a central registry for offenders." Poppy chuckled dryly.

"Sorcha set it up when she was Cesar's PA," Pia recalled, trying to hide her shock and alarm. "It's the kiss of death." A firmly closed door by the Monteros was a firmly closed door against the social and financial advantages that came from circulating in Spain's wealthiest circles.

Pia had presumed that her baby's father had been an invited guest to the ball and therefore had been vetted for casual association. Given his willingness to pay so much for the painting, he had to be wealthy. That meant he might not be her mother's first choice, but he was of suitable rank and standing that he would be accepted despite the unconventional circumstances.

Instead, he was an outsider who'd just been blacklisted.

"So what are you auctioning?" Poppy asked.

"Pardon? Oh." Pia wasn't one to lie. She rarely got herself into a situation where it was necessary, only the occasional prevarication over whether a meal had been enjoyed or a dress suited. "I have a few art pieces I want to place in their next catalog," she hedged. "My life will change as my academic career ends."

As she sat with her upturned hands stacked in her lap, cupping the air where her belly would swell in a few months, she debated whether to confide fully in Poppy. Poppy had been in nearly this exact position when she'd been pregnant with Lily.

But Pia had learned a long time ago that whining about a problem didn't solve it. Obstacles weren't to be mentioned until she had formulated a plan to overcome them—at which point her solution would be critiqued for merit and edited as necessary.

She wanted to cry, but rose instead.

"It's growing late. I'd rather not drive in the dark. Would you mind not mentioning to Mother that I came out today? I cut our lunch short, said I wasn't feeling well."

"The lunch with...?" Poppy gave a little sigh as she rose. "Pia, I don't want to speak out of turn, but are you sure an arranged marriage is right for you? Look at your brothers."

Pia couldn't help her small snort of irony.

"Please don't take offense, Poppy, but yes. Look at them. When Cesar married Sorcha, he threw over a long-standing agreement that would have paid a family debt." That relationship was in tatters and so was the one from Rico's first marriage, not that she had the poor taste to mention it, but everything Rico should have gained from that marriage had since been lost when it was discovered he had had Lily with Poppy.

Poppy paled anyway, forcing Pia to do something completely uncharacteristic and reach out to squeeze Poppy's arm.

"I consider both of you dear friends. Your children are a gift," Pia told her sincerely. "I'm pleased my brothers are in fulfilling relationships, but you've seen enough of our family's inner workings to understand the expectations placed upon all of us. On me to be the last bastion of rational behavior. I *have* to make a good marriage or brand the Monteros as impulsive and inconstant forever."

"You're expected to pay the price for our happiness?" Poppy asked. "That's not fair. Or rational."

"Perhaps not." But she wasn't supposed to bring further detriments to the table, either. "I'm not like my brothers, Poppy. I'm not built to go against the grain." One wild night notwithstanding.

"Women never are," Poppy said with a spark of defiance. "I didn't tell Rico about Lily for a lot of reasons, but deep down I know fear was the biggest thing that held me back. This…?" She waved at the mansion she had restored with impeccable taste. "Fitting into your world has been hard and terrifying and I know I'm making mistakes every single day. But it's worth pushing myself to be more than I ever imagined I could be to have what I have with Rico. My only regret is that I didn't tell him sooner, so we could have been happier sooner."

Pia forced a careless laugh. "Happiness is fleeting, Poppy." Where had she heard that before?

"I mean that we could have been together sooner. In love sooner. Which makes us happy." Poppy frowned with concern. "I know you weren't raised to expect a marriage based on love, but it is possible to find it, Pia. Do you want to be married to someone else when you do?"

"Food for thought," Pia said to end a discussion that was a lot more complex than Poppy realized. "I'll see you at Christmas."

But she drove home with white knuckles, mind churning over words that had struck particularly deep.

My only regret is that I didn't tell him sooner.

CHAPTER FOUR

ANGELO HAD READ the note so many times in the three days since he'd received it that he'd memorized it. Nevertheless, he read it again.

Señor Navarro,
We met at my brother's gala in mid-October. Would you have time for a brief conversation?
If your preference is the same as you stated at our previous meeting, I will respect your wishes and you won't hear from me again.
My contact details are below.
Sincerely,
Pia Montero, MSc.

No hint of the passion that had exploded between them. In fact, if he were to pick up this card from a desk or mantel, he wouldn't have any sense that something intimate had occurred between the parties concerned. It came off as a desire to reopen a business discussion, little more.

Which made him suspicious. Was she trying to draw him out? How closely linked was she to Tomas and Darius? Had she confirmed to them that Angelo had been on the former Gomez estate that night?

Angelo had no doubt that was how she'd learned his name. His brothers had thought they could disrespect and discard his mother one more time, but Angelo had ensured their disregard backfired.

He glanced at the painting of his mother. Freshly cleaned and newly framed, it hung over the safe that held the jewelry he had recovered. He had thought the portrait lost in the cottage fire. He would have paid any amount for it, but what made its acquisition truly priceless was the fact his brothers hadn't received a penny from his purchase. Given what he'd heard from the auction house, they were incensed they hadn't thought to extort him for it themselves.

As far as they knew, however, an agent had obtained it for him. They had no proof he'd been at the estate in person.

Unless Pia had said something.

This sudden communication from her could be a trick to force his admission that he'd been there that night.

Given that possibility, Angelo had taken the precaution of having her properly investigated, but there was little in the report that he hadn't read online.

Her age or educational history had to be mis-stated. Only a genius could earn a master's degree in environmental science before she'd turned twenty-one, after a double major in biology and chemistry and a minor in sociology. Three short years later, she was about to defend a dissertation analyzing polymer deterioration on barnacles and bivalves.

That was tomorrow, Angelo noted with a glance at his calendar icon.

This report wasn't telling him what he really wanted to know: Why was she contacting him *now*? Had it taken her that long to find him?

Even more salient, why had she made love

with a stranger that night? *That* question had been driving him mad.

Some people enjoyed conquests. Angelo's father and brother, for instance. He would normally think her targeting him had been a move from a fortune hunter, but aside from her own healthy coffers, he couldn't fathom how she had known he would meet her on that rooftop.

She had compromised him once he was there, though. The fact he'd given in to impulse and dallied with her, putting himself in real danger of being caught with his pants down, made her a weakness he should avoid.

He still didn't understand why he'd been so compelled by her. The high of his caper? The erotic circumstances of intimacy with a stranger? The sexy feel of his costume?

He sneered at himself and went back to scrolling through the report, finally seeing something new—speculation that she was in the early phases of finding a husband. Only *titled* bachelors with fortunes and impeccable reputations need apply.

Angelo pushed away from his desk, glad his damned brothers weren't on the shortlist, but it still disgusted him. If she was shopping for a husband, this card of hers wasn't an invitation to rekindle things. She *had* to be working with his brothers.

Nauseated, he picked up the note and studied her clean, level script. It would be easy to send word that she was mistaken; they had never met.

If she was operating on their behalf, however, it was exactly the closing of ranks and exertion of influence that had allowed his father to victimize his mother without consequence. He wouldn't let any of them get away with that again.

He messaged his pilot to ready his jet for Valencia.

Over the years, Pia had taken classes in public speaking and presenting. She had even gritted her teeth through an improvisation class to learn how to roll with the unexpected. Nothing had fully extinguished her discomfort in speaking to a group, but she had developed coping techniques, like picking out one or two unthreatening faces and pretending the rest didn't exist.

As for presenting and defending her material, her expertise in that had been honed during every family dinner from the moment she had joined her parents in their dining room at eleven. Speak clearly. Make her point in as few words as possible. Back up her position with supporting facts when required. Emotions proved nothing. Move on.

Since she didn't expect her audience to consist of more than the committee, the chair, her mentor and a few fellow students monitoring the procedure as they prepared for their own defense, she presented her dissertation in a small conference room off the university's faculty lounge.

After she attached her laptop to the projector, the chair introduced her.

"Thank you." She began her prepared remarks with a surface smile toward the committee and swept it around the room to find her two receptive faces.

Oh Dios.

Since visiting Poppy last week, Pia had quietly and obsessively researched Angelo Navarro. He claimed to be Spanish born, but had spent several years in America and now had homes around the globe. His childhood remained a mystery, but the story of how he'd made his recent fortune was everywhere.

After a few years in low-level jobs setting up video game equipment, he had hustled his way into promoting championships. That had led to partnering with tech entrepreneurs and gaming nerds to develop microprocessors for faster gaming. One of those patented chips had made its way into all the top smartphones and, three years ago, his team had accidentally created another chip that was now revolutionizing artificial intelligence.

He'd since begun offering high-speed cloud services that were expanding faster than a cumulonimbus on a humid summer's day and held untold reserves in cryptocurrencies. He probably buried gold bullion on his private tropical islands, too.

Pia had studied his photo, comparing it to her memories of a shadowed visage and a stubbled jawline beneath the edge of a mask, but in person he was even more fallen-angel-beautiful. His black hair gleamed. His eyes were utterly mesmerizing with their aquamarine color, crystal clear and piercing as he stared back at her, smug at having taken her so unaware.

She didn't need visual proof this was her mystery lover. She *felt* him. Felt the impact of being in his presence. Her heart hammered like a dull ax behind her breastbone—once, twice, three times. The careful tending of her diet to hold morning sickness at bay threatened to have been for naught.

Her falter lasted only those few heartbeats while she accepted that she was on a ship that had struck an iceberg. The galley was on fire and sharks were circling in the water. Panic was not an option. *Roll with it.*

She accepted the premise. This wasn't what she had expected or planned, but she wouldn't give him the satisfaction of rattling her. She made him one of her points of contact, using this opportunity to show herself as confident and knowledgeable because, in this narrow milieu, she was. She found a smile and made her purpose clear to everyone in the room as she began working through her presentation.

She compartmentalized, pulling a steel curtain across the messy gush of emotions that would need every type of mop, bandage and stitches later, when she was in a position to let down her guard and process what was happening.

The hour went by quickly. Suddenly she was shaking hands with the committee, having earned a doctorate and a grade of Excellent. She should expect a *cum laude* distinction, one informed her on the sly.

"I imagine your father will be very proud," her mentor said. "I would have thought your whole family would turn out for this."

Pia didn't mention that her father, a PhD himself, had a copy of her dissertation and would provide notes over Christmas with the expectation that she would incorporate them before final publication.

"They were tied up," Pia murmured as a tingle like radiant heat accosted the right side of her body.

He hadn't been wearing that cologne at the

ball, but she recognized his scent all the same. Her throat flexed with the effort of maintaining her screen of calm as she turned to face him.

"Señor Navarro," she said, offering her hand.

"Angelo," he corrected. His clasp sent electricity through to her nerve endings as he took the liberty of greeting her with, "Pia."

"Thank you for coming," she said, desperately pretending they were strangers when all she could think about was how his weight had pressed her into the cushions while her entire being had seemed to fly.

"An informative talk." His eyes dazzled, yet pinned her in place. There was an air of aggression about him. Hostility even, in the way he had appeared like this, when she had literally been on the defensive. He seemed ready for a fight.

She had almost hoped he would leave her hanging after her note. She could have raised their baby with a clear conscience that she had tried to reach out while facing no interference from this unknown quantity.

As for what would happen if he did get in

touch? She had tried to be realistic in her expectations, but Poppy had stuck a few delusions in her head. They seemed even more ridiculous as she faced such a daunting conversation with him. How had she even found the courage to say such frank things that night, let alone *do* the things they'd done? Wicked, intimate, carnal things that caused a blush to singe up from her throat into her cheeks.

"I need a moment," she said, voice straining.

She had already declined invitations for drinks, fearful her avoidance of a glass of champagne would make her condition obvious. She only had to say a last goodbye to the committee and, "Thank you again, but I must take this meeting."

Moments later, trembling inwardly, she led Angelo into the small office off the lab where she had worked the last three years when not in the field. She had already packed her things into a small cardboard box that sat on the chair. She was shifting from academic work to motherhood and marriage. That was all that was left of her former life.

Angelo seemed to eat up all the air as he

closed the door behind him and looked at the empty bulletin board, the box of tissues and the well-used filing cabinet.

Pia started to move the box, but he said, "I'll stand."

He was taller than her, which made him well over six feet because she had the family's genetic disposition toward above average height. His air of watchfulness was intimidating, too, especially when he trained his laser-blue eyes on her again.

"Your card was very cryptic," he said.

She had spent a long time composing it, wondering why he had sneaked into the ball when he could easily have afforded the plate fee. At the time, she had thought his reason for being on the rooftop was exactly as he had explained it—curiosity. She had many more questions now, but didn't ask them yet. There was every chance she would never see him again after she told him why she had reached out.

Memories of their intimacy that night accosted her daily. It was top of mind now, which put her at a further disadvantage. Her only recourse was to do what she always did when she was uncomfortable—hide behind a curtain of reserve and speak her piece as matter-of-factly as possible.

"I'll come straight to the point." She hitched her hip on the edge of her desk and set her clammy palms together, affecting indifference while fighting to keep a quaver from her voice.

"I'm pregnant. It's yours."

Angelo took it like the sucker punch it was. He jerked his head back in reflex and physically rocked on his heels to recover his equilibrium.

"*That's* the reason you tracked me down?" What about his brothers?

"It seemed a significant enough reason to. And I know what you're going to say." Her lashes swept down and her mouth tightened. "I take full responsibility. I had what I thought was my cycle the next morning so I didn't consider taking any precautions. Feel free to mock my extensive education in biology."

The silence ticked out for a full minute as he absorbed news that changed his life. All he could wonder was why he wasn't *more* shocked.

Probably because he'd had sex without protection, same as she had. He didn't need anything but adolescent whispers to know this was exactly the consequence he had risked that night. Only an adolescent would behave that recklessly and *not* expect this outcome. He wasn't a teenager. He had known the risk he was taking and he'd done it anyway.

He didn't let himself ponder why.

He did try to manufacture skepticism and searched for reasons to be suspicious, but he couldn't even scrape up anger. They'd both been rash. This was the result.

"Who else knows?"

Her amber eyes flashed up, appalled. "No one." As if the thought of anyone knowing was far too compromising to admit.

He ignored the sting of that and tried very hard to imagine how she could have known he would be at the ball that night, let alone got to the rooftop ahead of him. How could she have tricked him into unprotected sex so she could present him with this outcome, all in league with his brothers?

While managing to look hideously ashamed of it?

"It's been confirmed?"

"I have the result from the doctor's blood test." She started to reach for her purse, but he flicked a hand to indicate proof was unnecessary.

"I believe you." Given her discomfiture and the effort she'd made in tracking him down, he didn't think she would have told him unless she was sure it was his.

"I'm keeping it," she stated, voice cool. "I felt you should know, but this doesn't obligate you. I'm more than capable of supporting myself and the baby."

He searched her aloof veneer for the woman whose sexuality had been so tuned to his own they'd made a baby within minutes of meeting each other. Where was the goddess who'd set the bar so high he hadn't looked at another woman since?

"You're free to walk away if that's your preference." She glanced toward the door in what smacked of a dismissal.

"You think I would turn my back on my child?" That annoyed him. *His* progeny would never be something shameful to be shipped away to a penal colony of a boarding school, never recognized or provided for.

Her brows lifted with surprise. "Given our no-strings agreement, I anticipated your interest would be low to nonexistent."

"You anticipated wrong." His harsh tone made her stiffen, but she offered a jerky nod of acknowledgment.

"Very well. I suggest a trust. I'm in the fortunate position of being able to offer the child a comfortable upbringing without prevailing on you. It's really about what you consider a fair arrangement for the long term."

"Prevail," he insisted, his attention caught by her use of *the*. Not *our* child or even *my* child. *The* child. "I want and expect to be fully involved," he stated without equivocation.

"I see." Another blink as she absorbed that, cheeks hollow. "Well, we have time to discuss exactly how that will look. My wish is that we remain as discreet as possible while we work that out."

"You don't want anyone to know I fathered your child?" He wasn't shocked. She was a pedigree show dog caught in heat by an abandoned mongrel. He deliberately cultivated the image of a low-rank plebeian on an upwardly mobile trend as he infiltrated the establishment. All the better to annoy his noble brothers, but, "Why tell me at all if you want it to be our little secret?"

"I considered not telling you," she admitted frankly. Damn she was cool, perched so still on the edge of the desk, projecting patient tolerance of his presence before her. "But both of my brothers learned belatedly that they had children. I extrapolated that you might also feel cheated if such news came to light well after the fact. By being open with you, I expect we can make adjustments to accommodate our joint participation in the child's life while mitigating otherwise-damaging rumors."

There was the *the* again. He choked on a humorless laugh. "You sound like you're still pointing at data and graphs. Speak like a human."

She sat taller, her chin coming up, but there was a flash of irritation in her gaze that he found very satisfying. It meant he was getting under her skin.

"I'm too smart to be in this position. So are you. It serves both of us to keep this as simple and quiet as possible."

"Consenting adults have affairs. Sometimes they slip up. This news won't hurt either of us." In fact, in the back of his brain, he was seeing how this new connection to the upper echelon of society could play out very much in his favor. Maybe that was her concern? "Are you trying to sideline me because of who I am? You don't want to be associated with me? Is that it?"

"I don't know who you are, do I?" she shot back. "I know your name. I know you sneak into parties to which you aren't invited, place wild bids on innocuous items, then lurk in private areas like a cat burglar, seducing strangers you catch unawares. Would you like to explain *any* of that?"

He narrowed his eyes. "I was under the impression the seduction was a mutual agreement."

She looked away and briefly touched the back of her neck before clasping her hands in her lap again. "It was," she allowed. "But it was impulsive and irresponsible."

"What happened to 'no regrets'?" What had happened to that introspective, intriguing woman he'd been so compelled to hold and touch and possess? He really had been on some kind of daredevil high that night. She *definitely* wasn't his type.

"Regret comes from wishing for a different outcome from the one you face," she said flatly. "The truth is, why you were there and who you are doesn't change the fact that I chose to behave in a way that will reflect badly on my family. I can't undo that, but for their sake, I intend to do everything possible to cast this in as least damaging a light as possible."

She really didn't know about his connection to the Gomez family. She couldn't, or she would be hysterical right now.

As he was processing whether that was a

good or bad thing, comprehension of what she was really saying dawned. With it came a flush of incendiary heat.

"You're getting married anyway." He was instantly and inexplicably furious.

She stilled, asking cautiously, "How do you know about that?"

"I know a lot of things." He didn't have a clue what was happening, not to himself or her. He moved forward on reflex until his knuckles were on the hard desktop on either side of her hips, the tip of his nose a hair's breadth from hers. "I'm not letting a stranger raise my baby."

"I can't help the state of our relationship, can I?" She set a hand on his chest, but didn't push him away. Her hand lifted slightly from his shirt, as if she found him too hot to touch. She wasn't as unaffected as she was trying to appear. Her breasts rose and fell unsteadily. Her eyes were huge, her pupils big enough to eclipse her golden irises.

"You know what I mean. I want my child, Pia. Full access, every single day."

It was fascinating to watch the burst of emotion behind her eyes, the light flush of pink beneath her skin while she fought to maintain her unaffected expression.

"Until July, I'm the only one with access. I suggest you take that time to reflect on whatever reasons you had for not wanting it known you were at my brother's that night. When you can react less emotionally, we can resume this discussion."

He was starting to see how she used fifty-dollar words to put distance between herself and others, but he didn't back off one iota.

"You're carrying my heir. My *blood*. I will not walk away. Not now, not ever."

His words had an effect. He was close enough to see how deep they struck, causing both a spark of something that might have been gladness, but it was swallowed by her flinch of anguish.

"Angelo." It was the voice he'd heard on a darkened rooftop, ringing with *want-but-can't-have*. Her fingers curled into his shirt. "I told you that night I have obligations. They're due sooner than this baby."

From the moment he'd seen her in the conference room, he had itched to get her like this, close enough to feel the heat beneath the frost that encased her.

"You have obligations to me now."

She shook her head, but her pleading eyes slid to his mouth.

As he recognized the craving in her gaze, he experienced a rush of pure, carnal lust. Exactly the same spell that had gripped him that night. Her lips were right there, parted and shiny. Her breath moved across his own in shaken pants.

He wasn't the martyr she seemed determined to be. He gave them what they both wanted, cupped the side of her neck and took her mouth with his, reveling in the blast of heat and hunger. Lightning and craving hit him like whiskey. Her unique flavor and satin textures were all he would ever need in this lifetime.

She softened with surrender, exactly as she had that night, feeding his swell of powerful greed.

He held back nothing as he ravaged her mouth, slaking weeks of thirst. Her mouth moved under his, melting and clinging. Her arm went around his neck, pulling him down even as he firmed his arms around her, pulling her off the desk to stand against him.

She was on tiptoe, her body long and taut against his, exactly as he wanted her. This was what he had been looking for in his online searches. This tactile sensation of silk shifting against heat, a slender back and the small, firm lobe of her butt cheek in his hand; the crush of her breasts to his chest and her thick hair in his fist, the citrus scent and the tentative greeting of her tongue when he claimed her mouth with a sweep of his.

A sudden thump against the window had him jerking his head up, his arms shifting to form a protective shelter around her.

Outside, a young man stooped to pick up a yellow disk and laughed as he walked away, thumbing toward the window as he called out, "People are making out in there."

Pia made a noise of anguish and slid out of his arms, took two steps away and kept her back to the window. She hung her face in her hands. "Did he recognize me?"

"What if he did? We were only kissing."

She shot him a stark look and he had to

agree. Given the pace of their last kiss, they would have been making love very soon. His body was starving to have her beneath him. He was tense and aching, restless as an animal on the hunt. Twitching like a creature with the scent of his mate in his nostrils.

"We can't do this." She plucked a fawn-colored overcoat off a hook.

"Not here," he agreed, taking the coat.

She hesitated, then let him hold it for her. She shrugged into it as though pulling on her composure, the sensual woman of moments ago gone.

What the hell?

She gathered her purse and started to shoulder a laptop bag. He lifted the cushioned strap off her shoulder and dragged it free of her arm, partly out of chivalry, partly to catch the shift of awareness that flickered in her eyes before she lowered her lashes and stepped away.

Interesting.

He looped the bag onto his own shoulder, then brushed aside her attempt to pick up the cardboard box. He glanced at the contents: notebooks and screen cleaner, a nameplate and a framed certificate of her master's degree. He realized she was permanently vacating this office and he was suddenly reminded why.

"We should go for dinner. To celebrate."

"Celebrate?" She was so taken aback that she stumbled in retreat.

Amusement gathered across his cheekbones. "Your doctorate," he clarified, adding dryly, "The baby, too, I suppose."

He hadn't fully processed her pregnancy. He would become a father next summer. Was it cause for champagne? It wasn't cause for anything less, he decided.

"We don't celebrate things like that," she said stiffly, buttoning her overcoat. "Today was a completion point in exercising my academic potential, nothing more. Given this pregnancy wasn't planned, I wouldn't call it an achievement of remarkable note, either."

Wow. Was she really made of ice or was her indifference a defense mechanism?

He pressed his hand over the seam of the door before she could open it.

She released the knob and pivoted to face him, lifting her chin. She was a nice height.

He wanted to kiss her again. Press her into that door and make love to her against it. Drain the tension from both of them so they could talk without every word feeling like a grenade lobbing sexual anticipation.

He resisted. He didn't even brush away the strand of hair caught on her eyelashes even though his fingertips tingled in anticipation of her warm, downy skin.

"This baby is a remarkable enough achievement that I won't let another man take credit for it." It was vow and warning combined. "*I* will be Papà. No one else. So you and I will celebrate our engagement."

She displayed no reaction beyond a tremble of her eyelids and a fade of color from her smooth complexion and soft pink lips. After a long, tense moment she swallowed.

"How long have you known who I was?" she asked.

"I guessed your identity before I was off the property."

"And you waited until *I* found *you* before you came to see me. Until I told you I was pregnant before you asked me to dinner. I bring more to a marriage than a womb, Angelo. I expect my future husband to want and value *me*. So, no," she said firmly. Frigidly. "I will not marry you."

"Oh, *querida*, you're right that you don't know me. You shouldn't have revealed your deepest fear." He enjoyed the subtle confusion of latent desire and wariness that came over her as he bent his elbow, looming as though he would kiss her again. "Marry me or I'll go straight to the press with a tell-all."

CHAPTER FIVE

DEALING WITH THIS man was like having a slippery grip on a slingshot aimed into her own face. He unsettled her. Worse, his kiss had completely undermined the control she needed to project. She was doing her best to pretend she'd already forgotten it, but he was *impossible*.

She would love to go home and regroup, but there was no telling if he was serious about spilling their story or not.

"Dinner it is, then." It was a basic negotiation tactic she had learned from dealing with her parents. Concede to something minor to buy time to work on her counterargument. "Where shall I meet you?"

"We'll go in your car. I had my driver drop me."

Her hatchback was perfectly serviceable for carrying rain gear and collection buckets to beaches. It achieved great mileage, was comfortable on long treks and slipped easily into four-wheel drive on a muddy track.

Apparently Angelo expected something sleeker and sexier. He looked at her with disbelief. "This is your car?"

She beeped the fob to prove it.

He stole the key and adjusted her seat as he climbed behind the wheel.

With Angelo's attention on traffic, she brooded on the fact he had known who she was all this time and hadn't bothered to get in touch. His indifference hurt to the point her insides felt raw.

Her brothers were so happy, so irrevocably in love, she had allowed herself to entertain, just for a brief second, that she might trip into something like it for herself, even though she knew it was unrealistic, especially with a man she barely knew.

After days of mulling it over, however, she had decided to risk learning whether she and Angelo had anything beyond lust between them.

The lust was in full force. She was still reeling from their kiss. And his bold personality was as overwhelming as she had recalled.

She, however, had hardly proved herself to be a thrill a minute, droning on with her dissertation and having to be told to "talk like a human." She had shown herself to be as boring as every man had ever judged her to be, so it was hardly a shock that he wasn't interested in anything but the baby and perhaps another quickie if she was going to be easy about it.

She felt stupid for imagining he had been searching for her and might have welcomed the arrival of her card. It wasn't like her to be naive and romantic. Life was a lot less hurtful when she kept her expectations low, calculated odds and formulated logical steps to achieve her goals. Investing hope and yearning for emotional regard only courted crushing disappointment. *She knew that*.

Which was what she was experiencing right now, her heart sitting under a thorny weight as she revisited his marriage proposal based solely on the fact she was pregnant with his child.

She had never expected to marry for love,

but she did expect to be a full partner with her husband. She brought wealth, reputation, intelligence and practicality to a relationship. She was well-groomed, articulate, and spoke several languages. She might not enjoy being the center of attention, but she could lead a team, run a household and organize the hell out of just about anything. She was a decent sketch artist and played guitar on beaches if someone else wanted to sing.

Sensible, gallant Sebastián would appreciate all of that and bring his own quiet strengths and runt puppies to the relationship.

While unpredictable, Angelo was all threats and demands and brain-erasing passion.

She hadn't expected that. Not the kiss or the conflagration that had engulfed her the night of the ball.

Having given in to that once was causing a huge detour in her carefully mapped life. She couldn't let him shake her off her footing any more than he already had.

Yet here she was, in the passenger seat of her own car, arriving where he had driven her. He handed her keys to a valet outside a newly built beachfront hotel with old-world wedding cake architecture.

She scraped herself together and asked facetiously, "This is your home?"

"I bought the chain last year and keep a suite in each of them."

The *one* time she resorted to sarcasm and all she got out of it was his *gotcha* smirk for her trouble.

"I thought your focus was electronics," she said in a not so subtle, *I know things, too* way.

"I've reached a level of success that forces me to diversify."

Find places to park his money, he meant. She tried not to be impressed. She came from money, but his story was the sort of rags-to-riches tale she couldn't help admire.

"We're going for dinner, aren't we?" she asked as he steered her from the entrance to the restaurant and toward the elevators.

"You led me to believe you didn't want us to be spotted together."

Moments later, he let her into a tower penthouse decorated in muted tones of gray and ivory. There was a full galley kitchen, a master and a smaller bedroom, a dining area, a workspace and a lounge. Two-story windows overlooked a beach populated with pale, English travelers seeking winter sun.

Pia stood at the windows and linked her fingers casually when she actually wanted to clutch her elbows and hug herself. She didn't enjoy confrontation, but she knew how to frame a dispute and debate it calmly and constructively.

"Marriage isn't possible, Angelo. Let's take that off the table and discuss how to make shared custody work." She hadn't even begun to imagine that possibility.

"It won't. We're marrying."

Apparently he was less versed in "discussing." She bit back a sigh.

"If you think threatening a scandal will coerce me, you're wrong. I'd prefer to avoid one, but we are an extremely formidable family." She knew her parents would support her in every outward way. She would just have to suffer the rest of her life with the unrelenting knowledge that they'd *had* to. "You'll fare better working with us, rather than against us, trust me."

"First of all, I don't. Trust you, I mean." He came to stand next to her, hands pushed loosely into his trouser pockets, shoulders relaxed.

She had a feeling he genuinely was at ease while she was only pretending to be.

"Secondly, if you think threats of ruin will scare *me*, you're wrong. Not because I think I'm impervious, but because I'm not afraid to lose everything I own to get something if I want it badly enough." He turned his head. He was both laughing at her and deadly serious. "Can you and your formidable family say the same?"

Her stomach lurched. "There are no winners in war."

"Then don't start one."

She looked back toward the horizon, mind racing while her body tingled with awareness of his. "I didn't think one moment would risk my freedom," she said, voice steady even though she was caught somewhere between disbelief and despair.

"Marrying a man your mother chooses for you is freedom?"

"Marrying you because you decree it certainly isn't," she shot back.

"I want to marry so our child will have immediate access to both its parents. What is your vision of parenthood? An army of nannies and off to boarding school the moment you can?" he guessed scathingly.

"No." It came out reflexively because it was the last thing she would do to her child, not after having experienced exactly that mass production approach to child rearing. "The child won't go away to school until he or she is old enough to make an informed decision about the benefits and drawbacks." She would be hands-on, hugging and steadying and probably smothering, but she would work on not being too helicoptery.

"Why do you say it like that? 'The child.' Why isn't it *our* baby?"

"He or she is not an object we own. Further, if I say 'my' baby, it implies that I'm excluding you from the decision-making process. If I say 'our' it implies we're a couple. 'The' is a neutral acknowledgment that *the* child is a person in his or her own right for whom we are charged with making decisions that affect his or her entire life."

He shook his head in bemusement. "You can take the scientist out of the lab..."

His chide shouldn't have felt like such an indictment, but it did. She refused to flinch, though, only said, "I don't plan on experimenting on *any* child, particularly my own. Marriage to a stranger comes with too many uncontrolled variables. There is little stigma these days in having unmarried or separated parents so I see no compelling reason to marry."

"Every relationship requires time to get to know the other person. Those variables can be identified and labeled and filed into one of your folders however you see fit. The only reason I will accept for you refusing to marry is that you are in love with someone else. Are you?" His voice took on a lethal note that made her stomach wobble.

"No. But I'm not in love with you, either."

"Yet," he shot back with a wicked grin.

Her heart lurched and she looked away, fearful he would read into her physical infatuation and maybe even glimpse how reluctantly fascinated she still was with him, standing there countering her arguments in sabre-like flourishes of sharp and steely words. She couldn't marry that!

Yet every night since meeting him, she had gone to sleep wondering about him, imagining things having gone a different way. Wishing. Yearning.

It was a passing phase. *Por favor, Dios.*

"Love is largely a romantic notion. I'm not a romantic." She wasn't allowed to be.

"I noticed," he said pithily.

She hid her flinch.

"The only reason you're balking at marriage is because your parents expect you to marry a milquetoast from a 'good' family with old money. I happen to be a reverse snob who feels nothing but disdain for those who inherit their wealth instead of earning it. But I'm willing to overlook that flaw in you."

So magnanimous.

"Remind me to show you what I've earned

from my patents in biofuels and recycling of recovered plastics." She showed him what disdain looked like. Her mother's blithe smile, right here, on her face. "My parents expect me to marry someone with an unblemished background who complements our business interests, yes. *I* expect to marry someone who shares my values and supports my aspirations, whether that be motherhood or scientific research."

She didn't know where that last bit had come from. She had resigned herself to giving up that part of her life and contributing to the betterment of mankind through—*blech*—charity galas and the patronage of scientists who were allowed to pursue their passion.

"I don't care how many microscopes you buy as long as you're there when *our child* gets a ribbon at school. Which reminds me. Why weren't any of your family at your thing today?" He waved a hand toward the dusk closing in beyond the windows. "A PhD is a big deal, isn't it?"

"Not in my family." It was more the price

of membership. "It's something we're capable of, so we do it."

"Everyone in your family has a doctorate? Attained at twenty-four?"

"My father was twenty-five." She looked at her nails. "My brothers were both twenty-six." And yes, she had pushed herself to squeak hers in before her birthday next month. It was the bargain she'd struck with her mother, to get it finished early so she could marry before her eggs went stale. She was quite proud of the accomplishment, but knew better than to expect a fanfare for it. It was enough to know privately that she had done better than everyone else.

"Your mother…?"

"Married a scientist so she doesn't have to be one."

"Ah. But you'd like to continue to be one."

"Yes," she said with growing certainty. "I've allocated the next few years to marriage and starting a family—"

"Such an overachiever, getting it all done in one day."

Hilarious.

"I should probably disclose, I don't possess a sense of humor. Dare I hope it's a flaw that is a deal breaker?"

His mouth twitched. "I'm just as happy laughing *at* as *with*."

She looked away, refusing to smile, even though she kind of wanted to sputter out a chuckle. The stakes were far too high, though.

"What's *your* vision of marriage, Angelo?" she asked, bracing herself as she pointed out, "You've had an hour to process this. I can't believe you're really prepared to marry a stranger."

"Believe it," he said implacably. "My father was garbage. He gave me twenty-three chromosomes and a lot of bad memories. I'll do better by my own child. A *lot* better. Full disclosure," he mocked, "I have a blemished background. Flaws you *will* have to overlook."

"What kind of blemish?" she asked warily.

Once again he gave her a look that was so penetrating it made her feel encased in ice, unable to move. After a charged moment, his expression changed from severe to dismissive. He contemplated the horizon.

"We'll discuss it another time."

Frustrated, she demanded, "When? After we're married?"

She hadn't meant to speak of it as though it was a fait accompli. She rubbed away the shiver his austere look had lifted on her arms.

"Look, I accept that you want to be a good father. For the baby's sake, I'm pleased. That still doesn't mean we should marry."

"Live together then? I'm not hung up on making it official."

"Oh? Why didn't you say so? I'll marry as planned and you can come live with us. One big happy family."

"You're right. Your sense of humor needs work."

"I wasn't joking."

"I'm a man with an open mind, Pia, but my tastes don't run to ménage."

"I'm still seeing a solution, not a problem."

"Let me spell it out. I'm possessive. Any man who lives with us will be skimming the pool. You and I will share one bed."

"Optimistic, too."

"You don't want to sleep with me?" He

hitched his shoulder against the window so he was facing her.

"Not something you hear often?" she inquired with a lift of her brows that she hoped conveyed disinterest.

"Not often, no. When I do, I accept it as the truth. Today..."

"Why would I lie?"

"I don't know." He studied her.

It took everything in her to hold his gaze and keep her uneasiness from reflecting in her face.

"How many contenders were there?" he finally asked.

"For what?"

"Paternity."

"Excuse me?" She was pretty sure she was insulted.

"You were right when you said we're both too smart to be in this position. The excitement of the moment got the better of us. I accept that. But in the cool light of day, you slipped up again and didn't visit a doctor for a precaution. Given your extensive education, you are *way* too smart to make such a simple miscalculation."

She didn't know where he was going with this, but she felt as though he was peeling layers off her as he did it. She wanted to run, but she had to stand there and act completely bored.

"So?"

"You're smart, but you're not experienced." He spoke in a tone of dawning realization.

"In what way?" Her stomach flipped over as she attempted to maintain her laissez-faire attitude. "The use of birth control? You're right. It hasn't come up."

"No? Why's that?" He had a look on his face that was both amused and bemused, as if he knew the answer while she still didn't understand the question.

"Because I haven't had to use it before." Obviously.

"Because you were a virgin," he concluded. He was smiling. Laughing at her. *Dios*, no.

"Why is that relevant?" she asked, as mortified heat climbed her cheeks.

"Because even with my vast experience, I

usually know a woman more than ten minutes before I'm making babies with her. I *always* know her name."

The air seemed to crackle and snap between them.

She clenched her teeth, not enjoying hearing about those legions of other women and refusing to examine why. "How many babies do you have?"

"Just the one." He nodded at her middle.

He seemed to take the opportunity to track his gaze all over her sage-green jacket and its matching skirt. She had chosen the knit skirt because it was comfortable while the jacket's turned-up collar lent her an air of polished authority.

He took in the rest while he was down there, skimming his gaze to her snakeskin pumps and back to the bronze lace of her camisole between the lapels of her closed jacket, then finally up to her eyes.

He hadn't even touched her, but she felt restless and lethargic and self-destructive. Ready to abandon sense and propriety all over again.

It was all the reason she needed to reject

him. He was far too dangerous, undermining her with a look. She couldn't live her entire life with that!

"You understand this baby has been conceived?" she asked frostily. "No further action is required."

He chuckled softly. "The question on the table is whether you *want* to."

"I've answered. I said, no thank you."

"Because you want to sleep with the overbred nob your mother has chosen."

Put that way, she dreaded it, but, "When the alternative is someone who casts aside modesty or decorum, I struggle to see the strength in your argument."

"I usually have enough decency not to have sex in public, but neither of us showed much decorum or restraint, did we? You gave up your *virginity*. It's very rare for couples to react the way we do, you know."

"Current levels of overpopulation lead me to believe lust is fairly common," she murmured with another examination of her nails.

"Not this kind of lust. It's extraordinary. Do you need another sample?"

His hand started to come up and she dropped her own, jerking back a step beyond his reach.

He scratched his cheek as he chuckled. "So jumpy."

She smoothed her embarrassed irritation from her brow. "Deep emotions, such as lust, are detrimental to a comfortable life. Destructive, even. As we've demonstrated."

"The damage is done, *querida*."

"So let's not compound it."

"Agreed." He straightened off the window. "Let's not bring anyone else into this child's life that doesn't need to be here."

"Certain people, like my family, are already in my life. They will be affected."

"What are they going to do? Disown you?" His pitiless gaze dismissed them either way.

Her chest constricted. No, her parents wouldn't yell or reject her, but she would lose her chance to win their approval. For once.

Was that what she was holding out for? As that unpleasant truth slapped her, she knew that Angelo had won. Their baby had won. She was no longer the child. She was the parent and it was time to give up the fantasy of earning her parents' affection and show the sort of concern and unconditional love that she'd longed for all her life.

Damn it.

"My mother will need to be informed," she said with defeat. "Immediately."

"I'll go with you," Angelo said as she exchanged a few brief texts with her parents and announced she would visit their home on the way to her own.

"It's not necessary." Pia dropped her phone back into her purse.

"It is." Angelo didn't need approval from her parents. From anyone, for that matter, but the influence her parents exerted over her shouldn't be underestimated.

Pia was such a mystery. Coldly analytical, then flaring hot. Fascinating, but frustrating.

She moved to the mirror in the hall and set her purse on the table as she searched through it. "My parents are aware of your name in relation to the painting. They'll want to know your motives. How you came to be at the ball."

"Tell them you invited me."

"I don't lie to them."

"Then tell them you had no idea who I was and made love with me anyway." He shrugged it off, sidestepping what she was really asking.

He would have to tell her eventually, but he would wait until she couldn't back out of their marriage. That was partly tactical, partly selfish. He wanted his revenge on his brothers and it would carry so much more flavor if he was marrying up. Marrying spectacularly well, in fact.

But his ever-present aversion to dredging up his mother's situation rose in him. He never discussed her with anyone, ashamed to admit what he was. He carried a lot of guilt, too. His very existence had contributed to her agony. He had burdened her and ultimately let her down. He hadn't seen her suicide coming, but should have. He hadn't had many resources at the time, but he should have done something. In his heart, he was convinced he could have stopped her had he been there.

Pia pensively refreshed her lipstick, casting him a look with her reflection.

"Is this the sort of marriage we'll have? One

where we keep secrets? Because I was prepared to start mine to Sebastián by telling him I was pregnant with another man's child. The least you could tell me is how I come to be refusing him." She began pulling the pins from her hair.

"Never say that name to me again," he suggested pleasantly, moving to stand behind her in the mirror.

He picked out a few pins himself, concentrating on releasing the twist without causing her any discomfort.

She held very still, eyes downcast, her exposed nape begging for the press of his lips. He combed his fingers through the mass, watched the play of light through the silken strands, enjoying the smooth caress between his fingers.

"I don't know what sort of marriage we'll have," he admitted. "Marrying and starting a family has not been on my radar. I spent most of my life rootless, my own security tenuous. Until a few years ago, I was in no position to support anyone but myself. When I finally began making money, it was buckets of it. I had to pivot to defend against a different kind of predator, not the kind who eat the weak, but the kind who challenge the strong."

He let his hands rest on her shoulders and lightly dug his thumbs into the tendons at the base of her neck. Like magic, the stiff, aloof expression on her face melted. She closed her eyes and her expression grew so sensually blissful, he nearly picked her up and carried her to his bed.

But he had to make her understand.

"Mistrust is ingrained in me. I don't know yet if you're friend or foe, Pia. I certainly have no illusions that your parents will be on my side."

Her eyes opened, the shadows in them difficult to interpret.

"I only know that you're carrying my child. That our child will need you. That makes you as much my responsibility as the baby is."

"So you don't trust me, but I'm supposed to trust you?" she asked huskily. "Even if you keep secrets?"

He smiled. "Your intelligence is one of your most attractive qualities. Do you know that?"

"Almost as high a compliment as having a great personality." She brushed his hands off her shoulders and moved away.

"I meant it as a compliment. Why compliment your looks when your beauty is obvious." Even when she was walking away. Her skirt was a hip-hugging knit that caressed her backside and thighs every time she moved. He'd been admiring it all afternoon.

She stood in the middle of the room, hand on her middle, expression tight, face pale. "We should go."

"Nausea?" Now he wanted to tuck her into his bed and cuddle her.

"It comes and goes. I have biscuits in the car that help."

"When do you see the doctor next? Any concerns?"

"None. Everything is normal. I have an appointment in the new year."

"I'll come." He was already looking forward to it.

"If you like." The chill was back. So annoying, but he soon learned she came by it honestly.

Marble floors gleamed beneath a chandelier of icicle-like crystals as they entered the Montero villa. A wide staircase led to a gallery where stark, contemporary art decorated the walls.

The butler directed them into a showpiece of a parlor, the sort of room Angelo had glimpsed as a child, but had been held back from entering by his mother's tense hand on his arm, her voice sharp with caution. It was not a place he had been welcome and, judging by the expressions on the Duque and Duquessa's faces, he was no more welcome today.

"Navarro," her mother repeated, glancing sharply between them.

"Pia's plus one at the ball," Angelo lied smoothly so Pia wouldn't have to. "I trust my generous donation made up for concealing our relationship."

"Relationship." La Reina's tone dropped to subarctic levels. "How did you meet? The university? I don't believe I'm familiar with your family."

"No?" Angelo countered, thinking La Reina had probably been marrying Javier about the time his grandmother had become his father's second wife. But he couldn't think about the dirty secrets from his past. Not now when he needed to be on the top of his game.

"Nemesis Tech," Javier identified as he shook Angelo's hand with a solid grip. "I've read of your developments with integrated photonics. The first light-based microchip to be commercially viable."

"The reason smartphones can do so many things at once without bursting into flames," Pia translated for her mother.

"My team gets all the credit," Angelo said smoothly. "I only backed the winning horse." And flogged it to any manufacturer with money, from smart toasters to NASA.

"Technology," her mother said with a tolerant smile as they all sat. "Perhaps an introduction to Cesar would be prudent." La Reina sent that to Pia in a not so subtle query as to why her daughter had brought a stranger into their home on short notice. One who had not defined his use of the word *relationship.*

"Introductions to the rest of the family will happen in due course." Pia was utterly composed, hands folded in her lap, voice lacking inflection, face unreadable. Much as she'd been when she had kicked him in the gonads with her news. "I'm pregnant. Angelo is the father. We'll marry as quickly as possible."

The ensuing silence was so profound that the click of the door broke it like a gunshot. The butler came up against the charged air as though he had hit a noxious cloud. He persevered through it to bring Pia's requested cranberry mocktini and Angelo's glass of Javier's private label brandy.

"Dinner as scheduled, *señora?*" the butler murmured as he set the drinks.

"Push it back until I inform you." La Reina waited until the door had been closed again. Her color hadn't risen. Her voice hadn't changed. She only prompted, "Javier?"

"The Estrada merger was an ideal fit for the fuel cell innovations Cesar is pursuing. Microprocessing is a different direction entirely."

Sebastián again? Angelo wondered if they realized he could buy that fool's enterprise a dozen times over and his next generation chip wasn't even on the market yet.

"Rico enjoys the challenge of a pivot." Pia spoke as though they were discussing the purchase of a car or some other innocuous detail. "Cesar will find ways to capitalize. Both of them have dealt with the unexpected before."

"They have," her mother agreed.

Another profound silence. Pia stacked her white hands. Her mother sipped her frosted glass of white wine.

"I understand the social ramifications," Pia said, spine never faltering from its finishing school posture. "We'll marry as quietly as possible. Remove to a honeymoon somewhere unobtrusive and return after the holiday party season dies down."

"I never agreed to that," Angelo cut in.

"To marriage? Then we put Sebastián off for a year," La Reina said to Pia, apparently enjoying a quick pivot herself. "It's only fair to his future heir that there be clear distinction. You'll go away, as you do, and we'll work out a suitable arrangement with…" She gave Angelo a disdainful nod.

His scalp nearly came off. "I didn't agree to some furtive, backroom ceremony that implies we have something to be ashamed of. We'll marry with a proper wedding where everyone we know is invited."

These people really knew how to allow a silence to do their talking. He looked from Pia's downcast lashes, to La Reina's pointedly raised brows, to Javier's disinterested sip of his brandy.

"Are you embarrassed that your daughter is pregnant by me?" Angelo asked Javier. It was a double-barreled question, one the older man neatly brushed aside.

"The children and the family's social standing are La Reina's bailiwick."

"Is that a yes or a no?" Angelo asked with more antagonism.

"Angelo." Pia's clammy hand touched his.

"When one is drawing the wrong sort of attention, one ought to mitigate the damage," La Reina said in a chilly voice. "Take control of the conversation and lower the tone, for instance."

He barked out a humorless laugh.

"Am I speaking too plainly? My child is not something indecent to be swept under the rug." A bastard. A stain. The product of a crime. No one was saying it, but he heard the labels from his past and felt each one like the whip of a belt.

"Keeping a low profile will benefit all of us, including the baby," Pia said.

"If you act like we've done something wrong, people are going to believe we have. No." He rose, too angry to sit here like one of these overcivilized relics clutching their pearls. "Speed up the timetable if you'd rather not be showing in our photos," he told Pia. "The sooner the better works for me, but we are giving this wedding every bit as much fanfare as you would with one of those interchangeable grooms on your mother's list. We'll announce our engagement with a press release *tomorrow*."

"Have you thought this through, Pia?" her mother asked as if he hadn't spoken. "Faustina's parents are backing your father's challenger because of Rico's situation with Poppy.

This reinforces accusations that Monteros lack moral fortitude."

"Maybe they do," Angelo interjected. "Given you don't want to recognize your own grand-child."

"I didn't say we wouldn't recognize the child. Of course the child will be a Monetero." La Reina sent a small frown of affront toward her daughter. "Pia."

The word was a signal of some kind. Pia stood.

"Angelo and I will iron out the details in private, but I wanted you to be informed. We won't stay for dinner. Thank you for seeing us."

Angelo was no stranger to being shunned and insulted and run off like a mangy cur. He didn't intend to hang around for more of the same, but he was astounded that Pia allowed herself to be dismissed like some panhandler daring to come to the door.

"Will you take me home or shall I ask Moth-er's driver?" Pia asked him, her face a blank mask.

Angelo shot one last glower at her parents. "I'll take you home."

CHAPTER SIX

"IT'S BEEN A long day. I don't want to go back to the hotel," Pia said when Angelo ignored her direction to turn into her street.

"We're not going to the hotel." He still sounded furious.

She bit back a whimper of helplessness, one limp, cold hand cradled in the other. It really had been a long day. She wasn't up to further confrontations. Nevertheless, she tried to explain. "That wasn't shame they were expressing."

"The hell it wasn't."

"It was damage control."

"Yes, your father's election prospects. *Quelle surprise.*"

"It's not about votes. Not the way you think. My father is actually a good politician. He's extremely well-read, believes in science and facts and weighs the costs and benefits very objectively. He's never swayed by special interests or emotional pleas and certainly not by suitcases full of cash, only by sound reasoning. It's in the country's best interest that he retains his seat. That becomes more challenging when his children are having babies out of wedlock every other year."

"*You're* ashamed," he accused.

"I'm embarrassed that I showed a lack of self-discipline." And that she had embraced longing and hope and other nonsensical ideals that weren't based in logic. Soon she would advertise that bad judgment on the big screen that her belly would become. "I failed to live up to expectations. No one enjoys failing."

"You failed to stand up for our *child*."

His words, his tone, caused a spasming clench across her chest. Guilt. Anguish. Resignation. It was so intense, she had to take a moment to breathe through it.

How did she explain there was no point in growing indignant with them? Demanding feelings when there were none?

He turned into a private airfield. A stab of panic struck.

"Where are you going?" Was he so angry that he was leaving her? She couldn't blame him, but the profound sense of abandonment that gripped her as she faced him climbing onto a jet and disappearing was nearly more than she could bear.

"*We* are going to my home."

She opened her mouth, but he was jamming the car into Park and flinging himself from it, handing her car fob to someone with instructions to drive it to her home.

Stunned, she didn't move until Angelo came around to open her door.

"I don't have any luggage." That wasn't entirely true. She kept a clean pair of jeans and a warm pullover in the back seat for weather changes in the field.

"We'll manage." He jerked his head at the waiting jet.

"Angelo." She sought to reason with him, but he cut her off.

"What the hell do you have to stay here for? They didn't congratulate you on our baby or your doctorate or your forthcoming marriage. They don't care about you so why would you want to do *anything* they tell you to do?"

Tears slammed into her eyes. She fought them back, fought back the clawing sensation in her throat and the sick nausea that roiled in her belly.

The sad fact was, these weren't tears because her parents overlooked her accomplishments or disapproved of her choice in a husband. This was a deeper anguish that aligned directly with the rejection he was feeling on behalf of their child.

She knew that injured anger so well. It hurt her that he was experiencing it. Hurt her that their baby might one day see it and feel it.

She looked at the jet, thought about how many times she had done exactly this— jumped on an airplane yet never quite managed to outrun this ache. Or had anyone chase her and tell her she was missed.

For once, however, she wouldn't be alone in her pain.

She cleared her throat and asked that her laptop and other effects be transferred aboard.

She waited until they were in the air, after they'd been served a light bisque with puff pastry and Angelo seemed marginally less incensed, to try to explain.

"My parents are not emotional people. They will never be happy about this baby because they aren't capable of it. If you expect an effusive expression of joy from them in response to anything, you will be sorely disappointed." She had had to learn that lesson over and over. It still hurt, but it remained true. "On the other hand, they aren't specifically *un*happy, either. What you witnessed was resistance to a course correction."

"Something I've witnessed twice today," he said darkly.

She fought letting him see how stricken she was to be likened to her mother, which only made her more like La Reina, she supposed.

"One doesn't achieve a goal by giving in the minute an obstacle is encountered," Pia said, her voice empty of the defensiveness squeezing her in a vise. "I had no idea how you would react to this. Of course I tried to preserve the life I had planned for myself. That's very natural and human."

His snort disparaged the bunch of them as any such thing.

"How will your family react?" she asked stiffly.

He flinched and turned his profile away. "I don't have any."

Given what he had told her of his father and his childhood, she had wondered. This was obviously a raw topic for him so she didn't go digging around, only ate the last morsel of lobster in her bowl.

"Mine may not be the most demonstrative family, but we are loyal. What you saw as sweeping under a rug, my mother saw as a genuine effort to shield the entire family from adverse consequences. *I* would prefer to marry in private," she added.

"I stand by my response. Ducking attention implies we have something to hide." He sounded immovable.

She realized her phone was blowing up. "Did we just come into range or something?"

"The pilot has turned on the Wi-Fi, yes."

She looked at the numerous texts and missed calls from her brothers, the notifications from the family lawyer, her mother's assistant, the family's PR manager and—*Really, Mother?*—Sebastián.

"Who is it?" Angelo asked with a frown.

"Everyone." She quit scrolling and considered turning it off, but Poppy rang through with a face call. Pia made the split-second decision to accept so she could test the temperature with her brothers.

"Why didn't you *tell* me when you were here? I'm pregnant, *too*," Poppy said.

"What?" Pia's brief soar of excitement fell away. "Are you crying?"

"Yes." Poppy laughed and wiped her eyes. "I had to ask Rico to put Lily to bed. She doesn't understand that you can cry from being happy and hormonal, but I totally broke down when he told me. I'm *so* happy. And I don't want to steal her thunder, but I would bet any money Sorcha is pregnant, too. I haven't seen her take so much as a nip of alcohol in weeks. This is so *perfect*, Pia."

It really wasn't, but Pia was pleased by Poppy's reaction. She congratulated her on her own pregnancy, then had to ask, "Is Rico upset with me?"

"Of course not. He's worried. But thrilled," Poppy hurried to clarify. "He's been on the phone to Cesar a few times. They want to talk to you. And Angelo." Poppy gave her a look that accused her of holding back.

Pia smiled weakly. "It's been a long day. Tell Rico I'll call tomorrow, after Angelo and I have had time to make a few decisions." She signed off.

"I like her," Angelo commented.

"I would challenge anyone not to," Pia said mildly, hiding the stab of jealousy that struck like a bolt of lightning out of nowhere.

They finished their meal and Angelo noted it was still early enough in California to call his lawyer there.

Pia closed her eyes, wishing she had been able to ask Poppy if she still thought telling her baby's father was the right thing to do. She wanted to ask how to cope with the conflict of being happy about the baby, but overwhelmed by how it was changing her life at a pace she couldn't adapt to. How to make things work with the father when she didn't know what sort of person he was or what he wanted from her.

Was she a fool to put any trust in him at all?

She didn't realize she had fallen asleep until she woke at the sound of her name.

A warm, blanketing sensation of well-being surrounded her as she dragged herself back to consciousness. She only realized as she picked up her head that she was tucked beneath Angelo's arm, her head pillowed in the hollow of his shoulder.

His other hand fell away from caressing her cheek to wake her.

"We can sleep in the stateroom if you're too tired to go to the house, but it's only ten minutes from here."

She nodded dumbly and gathered herself, asking as they disembarked, "This is your island?"

"It's often reported that I bought the whole island, but that's inaccurate. I own the largest property and I purchased several of the more modest homes for my staff because I often prefer to be alone in the house. But there are many holiday homes here. There's a busy village in the harbor and a variety of tourist accommodation."

A handful of staff welcomed them into the massive villa—maids and security, a butler and one of Angelo's personal assistants. The butler showed her around a modern mansion decorated in bone white and natural stone. The lounge was sunken off the dining area and the exterior walls were glass panels that opened onto the pool surround. The water glowed pale blue in the night and the pool was so big, there was a bridge to an island within its shallows. Three potted palm trees and a bistro table with tall stools sat upon it.

Beyond that, the wide stretch of white sand glowed in the moonlight. The shape of a cabana, a boathouse and a private dock were outlined in fairy lights.

"This is beautiful."

"One of my business partners, a security specialist, told me about it. He and his wife live on the other end of the island. You'll meet her tomorrow. I asked her to take our photo for the press release."

"You have a rooftop patio like Rico's," she noted as she turned to study the side of the house that faced the water. It was all flowing lines, elegantly placed lanterns and recessed stairways.

"Would you like to see it?"

It was dark and the wind off the water chilly. She hugged herself, mouth dry as she considered what had happened on the last rooftop. What was wrong with her that she wanted to do that again? She didn't know him much better at all.

At her silence, he let a slow smile form on his face until he was so wickedly beautiful, her stomach wobbled. He took her hand and she didn't balk as he led her through the house.

When they reached the top of the stairs, he motioned at an open door to a spare bedroom. "What do you need for your research lab? Concrete walls or just an office space?"

"I—" She was so surprised, her tongue tangled. One way or another, pursuing science had always been an uphill battle. Her father set high standards; her mother thought it a distraction. Sexism was rampant and her studies often took her to remote places that were a challenge in themselves.

She didn't know how to compute that Angelo would simply take her at her word that she wanted to continue to work and try to facilitate that for her. "I haven't given it much thought."

"Let me know," he said, and led her into the stadium that was the master bedroom—which further disconcerted her.

She tugged to free her hand.

"The lady knows what she wants." He spun to face her.

"I really don't." She folded her arms, taking in the cool blues of the bedding in the soft light cast by the two lamps on the nightstands.

"The access to the rooftop patio is off this balcony." The humor in his eyes told her he was teasing her. "Stay here or go up, either way we're in trouble." He held out his hand.

She didn't move, only glanced toward an archway into what looked to be a master bath of epic proportions. There was a cozy conversation area in the nook and a desk near the door to the balcony. Her laptop bag had been left on the rolling chair.

"Do you really expect me to sleep with you here tonight?" she asked with disbelief. "We've known each other two days."

He sent a pointed glance to the clock that read twelve-oh-seven.

"Technically three." He pushed his hands in his pockets, seeming all the more imposing in the intimate golden light. He angled his head to regard her. "I don't 'expect' sex. I anticipate it."

How did he send all these swirls and eddies into her middle with just a few words and a sexy smile?

"It doesn't have to be tonight." He stepped closer and slowly swept his fingers down her hair, the caress so startling and so powerful that she caught her breath. He left his fist resting on her shoulder clutching a swathe. His thumb grazed the edge of her jaw. "Why so nervous? We've done it before."

"Not with the lights on."

He threw back his head and laughed. "We'll start with only one." He nodded at the night table. "Work up to it."

She hated that he mocked her, made her feel so inept. She knew she wasn't the best at interpersonal relationships. Her upbringing had been a wasteland, her shyness crippling. In the last few years, while most people her age had been clubbing, she'd been immersed in school, partly as self-defense, partly for the sense of accomplishment before she devoted herself to motherhood.

The one time she had acted her age with an impulsive hookup, she'd blown her life to smithereens.

While he remained completely self-possessed.

"I don't know who I was that night," she said with as much dignity as she could muster. "I wasn't me. I believed that you didn't know who I was and that I would never have to face you again. I didn't expect to reckon with the way I behaved. Now I'm forced to and it's not comfortable."

His hand shifted to gently pick up her chin and coax her to look into his sobered expression.

"There was nothing wrong with the way we behaved. Yes, we could have been more responsible, but sex is normal. Actually, our sex was exceptional in the best possible way," he allowed. "*I* don't feel embarrassed by it."

She doubted he was ever embarrassed, he was so confident.

"You don't understand," she murmured. How could he? He hadn't been raised to believe that corporeal yearnings were to be ignored and overcome in favor of rational decision-making.

"I'm not going to pretend I don't want to make love to you. I do." He set his hands on her hips, his touch heavy and possessive and stirring her without even trying. "If you don't want to, I'll survive." His thumbs pressed with tension into her pelvic bones while his mouth curled into a wry smile. "But you're right that we need to get to know one another. That won't happen living in separate quarters of the house. I want to share a room and a bed, if not our bodies."

What about talking? She didn't have much skill or practice at expressing her feelings verbally, though. She had never been allowed to acknowledge them and work through them.

As for the physical... He had held her closer

when they had danced that night, but she was experiencing the same pull now as she had experienced then, without the magic of moonlight and music and disguises. She was baffled by her reaction. She set her hand on his chest, maybe distantly thinking to give herself some space to think, but her fingers splayed to take in as much firm muscle as she could. She could feel his heartbeat and it chipped away at any attempt at rational thought.

He moved his hands to her waist, his touch a caress. An invitation to move closer. She stiffened slightly as tingles of pleasure wafted through her.

He lifted his hands off her so only the heat radiating from his palms touched her. "No?"

She wavered. She had spent her life drowning in a dry sea and his touch was a lifeline so compelling and welcome, so powerful, that she yearned for him, but she didn't know how to tell him she wanted him to touch her. It felt like a weakness to need it so badly.

Her body spoke for her, flowing without conscious volition. Her hand slid up behind his neck while her other arm reached to encircle his waist. She closed her eyes, not wanting to see how he reacted, only pressed herself to his front and lifted her mouth in offering.

His mouth landed on hers, sending a ball of heat into her middle while his arms closed across her back, pressing the air from her lungs. Maybe she forgot to breathe. She didn't care. She only wanted this. The uncivilized taste of him and the way her muscles quivered in response.

When he dragged his head up, she whimpered in protest.

"Open your eyes." His hand cradled her jaw, oddly tender when he was holding her in such a hard clasp, but maybe he was holding her up.

She blinked her eyes open, watched him slowly smile at whatever dazed sensuality was clouding her gaze. It was so intimate that her eyes grew wet. She could barely stand it, but couldn't look away. Her blood pounded in a primal, painful beat.

"I wanted to see that," he whispered. "What I do to you."

"It's too much."

"But you'll come to my bed anyway."

"I will," she capitulated, and gasped as he swept her up. Two steps later, he set her on the mattress.

He came down with her, his mouth swooping to possess hers again, ravenous. She tried to keep up, unable to pull apart the sensations that bombarded her. A whisking touch, a tender nibble and the abrasion of his cheek as he went after her neck. The sudden skim of his fingers against her thigh would have been more shocking if she hadn't somehow pulled his shirt free and was mindlessly brushing her palms across his bare back.

His muscular body, hard as iron, half pinned her, and his eyes filled with shifts and flashes when he pulled back enough to look at her again.

Fascinated, she watched his face as he lifted and found the catch that belted her jacket. Slowly he worked the buckle free and opened the front, settling beside her as he revealed her bronze camisole with its matching bra beneath.

"This is what I wanted time for that night." He flattened his hand on her stomach, shifting hot-cool silk across her torso, bending to nuzzle where lace met quivering skin. "To undress you."

He tugged at a sleeve and she pulled her arm free, then draped it across his shoulders, fingertips seeking the heat beneath his collar at the back of his neck.

She learned the difference between expecting and anticipating as she offered her other sleeve only to have him kiss the inside of her wrist, settle his mouth over hers in a way that drugged her into a mindless state and then, when she was trembling, he finally pulled her other arm free.

Hardly anyone had ever seen her this naked and only her jacket was gone. It wasn't just the lack of clothing that was revealing so much as the way her stomach quivered and her nipples pressed against the cups of her bra, and how her hips angled into him the way leaves of a plant sought the sun. Her desire rose so fiercely that she dampened silk he couldn't see and bit her lip against a groan of erotic suffering.

He was killing her, looking at her, biting against lace, slipping a strap down her shoulder, lifting to watch the slither of silk as he drew it up and away.

The way he ate up every inch of skin he exposed bolstered yet destroyed her. And the way he roamed his hand across her, from hip to the underwire of her bra, back down to her navel, then up to trace the swell of her breast against the edge of the cup, turned her inside out.

He began to devour her, stubble scuffing her chest while he teasingly bit at her nipples through the bra before he trailed his tongue where his fingertips had been and delved behind the cup to flick at her nipple.

She made a keening noise and his hand hardened on her hip, urging her to withstand his teasing until he finally took pity on her and released her bra, helping her remove it. He returned to lave and nuzzle and suck, driving her so mad that she hitched her ankle around his and tried to insinuate herself beneath him.

He growled and scraped his mouth down her center, making her abs jump at the flick of his tongue into her navel. He groaned in pleasured satisfaction as he reached the waistband of her skirt and discovered it stretched easily to slide down her hips.

He set kisses on one hip then the other, and kept sliding down with a whisper of his body moving against the covers. As he revealed her panties, he trailed kisses down her thigh, making her melt. Making her burn.

"Angelo," she gasped, shaking with arousal.

"I want you naked this time." The skirt was tossed to the floor. "Completely naked. So all you feel is me." He began inching the lace down her thighs.

She pressed her legs together, trying to ease the aching between them, then met his gaze as he patiently waited for her to bite her lip, then relax to let him peel off the lace panties.

He rose onto his knees and tossed them away. Then he dragged at his own clothing, movements efficient, gaze traveling over her as he stood to remove his pants.

The wanting in her was back to being that wild, reckless thing that had gripped her the night of the ball. Voices of caution and shyness were drowned out by imperatives of an earthier nature. She wanted his weight. His hard heat moving inside her. His firm hands steadying her. His mouth ravaging hers.

She held up her arms, inviting him back.

He set one knee on the mattress, one hand on the inside of her thigh, asking her to make space for him. But as she hesitantly opened her legs, he pressed for a wide space and settled low between her thighs, like a lazy jungle cat. He made a noise somewhere between a growl and purr as he warmed her intimate flesh with a hot breath that made her sob. Then he leisurely tasted her.

She couldn't speak. Couldn't process this much pleasure delivered in such an intimate fashion. Couldn't understand how he made her feel fragile and feral at once. Greedy and flagrant and willing to give herself up to him completely. But the pleasure he wrenched from her was magnificent. Unstoppable.

"Angelo!" she cried as her climax lashed her, devastating her so she was nothing but panting ash.

He peeled her fist from his hair and bit the inside of her thigh, shocking her buzzing nerve endings back to life.

The animal craving to mate had her fully in its grip now. Her *mate* had her fully in his grip as he rose over her and thrust deeply, pressing a keening cry from her. She closed her legs around him, clinging on in a small battle of strength as he thrust with muted power.

The act grew wild as he scraped his teeth against her neck and she dug her fingernails into his buttocks, urging him to shed what control he retained. She wanted all of him. All of his heat and greedy hunger. All his strength. All his craving and all of the roaring beast within him.

Her vision paled and her breaths were nothing but jagged, helpless soughs, pleading for the crisis. They crested in the same moment, the world making one glorious, silent rotation as they were held on that beautiful precipice.

Then the universe exploded into colors and streaks of joy and every molecule in her body caught fire as she slowly fell back to earth.

CHAPTER SEVEN

ANGELO HAD THOUGHT he knew what he wanted—to burn past Pia's layer of reserve and remind her how they had ended up in this situation. Along the way, he expected her to quit acting like she was better than him. Then he would issue a press release announcing he was hitching his common bag of bones to one of the aristocracy's privileged princesses, dragging all of them down a peg. The photo of Pia wearing some of the stolen jewelry would be an especially insolent nose-thumbing to his brothers.

He hadn't expected his hunger for Pia to be outright insatiable. They had made love three times through the night, the third time when she woke him at dawn by sliding languorously against him. Her sleepy mouth had painted a path across his chest to tease his nipple. How was he supposed to resist that? As they'd rolled into each other and twined their limbs, he'd been hard and she'd been slick and ready. Their joining had been natural and lazy and so sweet his teeth still ached.

He wanted to be smug, he really did. Physically, she was an easy conquest, but damned if he wasn't easier. He had taken her apart and she had destroyed him right back, then managed to look very wan and delicate over breakfast, stirring protective instincts he hadn't known he possessed. She was avoiding eye contact and blushing and obviously so self-conscious about losing her inhibitions, he couldn't help but caress a knee here and kiss the inside of her wrist there and reach across to slide a tendril of hair behind her ear.

"Is that your journal?" he teased, not sure if he should be flattered or worried that she might be recording her thoughts and impressions of his performance last night.

"It's a data log of my pregnancy." She frowned as if that ought to be obvious.

No casual food diary for Dr. Pia Montero. She proceeded to show him how she ruthlessly recorded caloric intake and nutrition, her morning weight and hours of sleep, physical measurements, the supplements she was taking, type and duration of exercise, and general notes on symptoms, physical and mental, including what time they occurred.

"Why?" He estimated this would take an hour of her day for the next thirty-plus weeks.

"I'm a willing subject. Why wouldn't I make an effort to contribute knowledge and understanding of a condition that affects the majority of women, directly or indirectly, at least once in her lifetime?" She blinked owlishly behind a pair of glasses that were provoking serious librarian fantasies in him.

"Aren't you turning it into more work than pregnancy already is?"

"Recording my observations relaxes me."

Did she realize how much she revealed with that remark? He could have asked what she could possibly be nervous about, but she was so earnest as she noted every detail of their baby's life as it formed within her that he found himself suppressing a rueful grin. Especially because she wasn't doing it to impress him or anyone else, but for womankind in general. He couldn't mock her for that.

Which made his own goal of highlighting the farce that was her noble birth seem petty and misguided.

He clung to his ambition until he began setting out the jewelry on his desk, when his desire for retaliation began to be smothered beneath a wave of revulsion.

"Family heirlooms?" She scanned the ostentatious pieces. Most were reflective of late twentieth-century indulgence. Intricate pendants hung from thick chains of yellow gold. Layered pearl necklaces were bedecked with amethysts and emeralds.

"This reminds me of the royal engagement ring." She touched a pair of blue sapphire earrings surrounded by white diamonds.

Angelo had to resist pulling her hand away, as though she were a child reaching out to touch a hot stove.

In the height of his anger after leaving her parents' home, he had coldly calculated that he would dress Pia in the extravagant white diamond choker with the matching bracelet.

It was a notable piece that some elderly contemporary of his grandmother's might glimpse and recall, causing the first stir of rumors. Definitely his brothers would recognize it. He had planned an ambiguous headline saying something about the secrecy of their relationship coming to light—one that would incite panic that a darker family secret was about to be revealed.

But the thought of these blood diamonds touching the smooth, fragrant skin he had tasted and stroked through the night sent an oily sensation into the pit of his gut. *No*. Just, *no*.

"I don't wear jewelry as a rule." Pia eyed the enormous, pear-shaped diamond in a platinum setting. Sprays of diamonds came off either side. Her impassive expression was the furthest thing from covetous. "Rings and bracelets get in the way when I'm reaching into tide pools and necklaces get caught on the microscope. I appreciate that these have special meaning to you. I'll wear something for the photo if you insist, but I've never been one to adorn myself. I'm hideously practical that way."

"I'm glad you hate it," he said flatly.

"I didn't say that!"

"Excuse me, Angelo. The stylist is here," his PA leaned in to say. "And Mrs. Killian."

"Call the jeweler in the village," he instructed. "Ask him to bring his engagement rings. Immediately."

"Yes, sir."

"Angelo—"

"It's fine," he said abruptly, not examining whether his veering from his plan was a sign of weakness or principle. "Melodie." He greeted his neighbor and introduced the highly sought-after photographer to Pia, then waved at the jewelry he'd left on his desk. "I have a second assignment for you. Photograph these for an auction catalog."

He tipped the empty tin so his toy wolf and race car fell into his palm with a wrapped hard candy his mother had sneaked to him twenty-five years ago. He had wanted to save it for a special occasion, but hadn't been able to get back to the rooftop to retrieve it. It went into his pants pocket with the toys before he swept all the ill-gotten jewelry back into the tin.

"Oh. Where...?" Melodie was startled as she accepted the heavy tin. She looked to Pia, who pasted on her most inscrutable smile.

"Your house is Fort Knox," Angelo reminded Melodie. Her husband had wired this one and was probably the only person on earth who could break in and steal that box if he wanted it. "Take it to your studio and get to it as your time allows."

Pia was utterly perplexed by Angelo's behavior. One minute he'd been her indulgent lover, touching her across the breakfast table in casual affection that soothed the constant ache of emptiness inside her. She had needed that reassurance after a night of completely immersing herself in the pleasure he gave her. She felt stripped raw by their passion. The winter sun stung her scorching skin and gave her no place to hide as he looked at her with a knowing, wicked grin.

She had buried her nose in her notebook, right back to boarding school, using research and reporting as a place to hide.

Then he'd brought her into his office, "To find something to wear."

He said nothing about the portrait that hung behind his desk. The canvas had been gorgeously restored so the subject was hauntingly pretty and maybe even familiar?

She hadn't had time to compare his mature, masculine features to the soft, youthful feminine ones. He had distracted her by producing a fortune in jewels jumbled together in a cheap tin. He poured them out as if spilling marbles on a play rug.

What she had said had been true. She found jewelry more of an encumbrance than something she enjoyed wearing, but the pieces had also been very—she cringed inwardly—flamboyant. Not just a statement of wealth, but a tacky neon sign declaring it.

She hadn't meant to reject it, though. Being in any sort of intimate relationship was new to her and she walked a tightrope of wanting to preserve her sense of self while maintaining some of the closeness they'd found through lovemaking. They would have a much better foundation for communication and understanding if he wasn't keeping secrets from her, but she wound up feeling she was the one who had damaged their delicate bond when he swept everything away and ordered the jeweler to bring a different selection.

Now he was marching around the house with Melodie, discussing where they should take their engagement photo, providing no opportunity to reestablish their connection.

He decided on the lounge and Melodie began setting up her equipment.

Pia followed Angelo to the guest room where the stylist excitedly pulled selections that were nothing like Pia's usual earth tones.

"She's right," Angelo said as the woman held a dress to her front. "That blue brings out your eyes and makes your skin look like honey."

Flustered by what sounded like an effusive compliment, Pia tried on the sleeveless dress. The circular neck strap that formed the collar lent an air of sophistication while her bare shoulders kept it feminine.

Since the rest were even sexier and more attention grabbing, she accepted the blue and sat for her hair and makeup. She only endured this level of fussing for the occasional gala, but always insisted on a light hand.

"A natural look, I understand," the stylist assured her. "You hardly need anything. I wish I could duplicate this glow of love with cosmetics. It's all a woman needs."

A shrink of panic pulled a chill into her center. There's no *love*, Pia wanted to protest. How could there be? This was the glow of a sexually satisfying night. Pregnancy, perhaps. Regardless of what it was, Pia didn't want it on display. Her emotions and self-worth and composure were delicate crystals in a snowflake, not the cast-iron reinforcements that most people possessed. She needed to protect herself at all times.

As the woman worked, however, her reflection grew more limpid and vulnerable, leaving her devoid of her usual shields. No dull colors, no bare face with glasses. No pinned-up hair and accoutrements like clipboards and notebooks. Her boring life typically left its stamp on her, but today she wore a flush of sensuality. Rather than the sophisticated, straightened hair she usually preferred when forced to dress up, the stylist had exaggerated her soft waves so the mass bounced as she walked.

"We're in luck—*I'm* in luck." Angelo's voice changed as the sound of her heels drew his attention. He straightened, very handsome in a bespoke dark blue suit, his tie not yet on. His rakish, casual air was in full force.

At his approving tone, everyone looked at her.

Melodie was at her tripod and the jeweler stood at the dining table, setting out rings on a black velvet swatch. Two of the servants hovered, Angelo's PA lifted her face from her tablet and the stylist came out behind Pia to agree enthusiastically with Angelo.

"Doesn't she make a beautiful bride-to-be?" the stylist gushed.

Everyone applauded.

Pia wanted to *die*.

It took every one of her twenty-four years of struggling to overcome her bashfulness to smile distantly and hold up her chin as she crossed what felt like a mile of hot coals to reach Angelo.

"You look stunning." The warmth in his

smile evaporated when she only offered a deliberately absent, "*Gracias.*"

Angelo introduced the jeweler, who had recently been to New York and had brought back a fresh selection for the well-heeled travelers who vacationed on the island.

"I thought this one? The setting wouldn't catch on anything," Angelo said impassively, offering a platinum-set, emerald cut diamond. It had to be three carats, but was remarkably understated despite the trapezoid cut diamonds on either side. The band was lightly brushed to give it a frost-kissed finish.

Pia looked at the ring and saw water in all its phases, from ice to glimmer to mist. Mostly, she was knocked off her feet that Angelo had heard what she'd said and was trying to find something that would work for her.

"Or this?" Angelo started to reach for another, but Pia couldn't take her eyes off the first ring. The last time she had experienced such a covetous desire for an object, she'd been looking at a two-man deep-dive submarine.

"I like this one."

He threaded it on her finger and, when it fit perfectly, another cheer went up.

A fresh flush of being too conspicuous and unguarded came over her. She tried to fight it, but Angelo surprised her with a kiss. His fingertip touched her chin, tilting up her mouth. In a smooth move, he captured her lips, casually flipping her into memories of the night they had shared. His other hand skimmed lightly across her bare shoulder, finding the exposed skin in a tickling caress as he gently brought her in closer.

No, she realized belatedly. She was the one who moved into him, trapping her own hands between them in her need to be closer while he warmed the back of her shoulder with his palm. Her fingertips reached to his jaw, begging him to stay close enough to allow her to continue devouring his lips while sensations tugged in her middle and her knees became liquid.

Distantly she heard a click and there was a flash behind her closed eyes. Melodie murmured, "That was the one, mark my words." The stylist tittered.

Pia blinked her eyes open and saw the flare of satisfaction in Angelo's, as though he had deliberately provoked her clingy reaction.

The magnitude of the moment struck her. She was *marrying* this man. Having his *child*. She would be under his power *forever.*

Shaken, she did everything she could to recover her composure, drawing back and smoothing a hand down her dress only to see a hard light come into his gaze.

Pia pretended she wasn't bothered and went through the motions for the rest of the shoot. All the photos were nice, but Angelo decisively chose, "The kiss."

The image on the back of Melodie's camera might as well have been a compromising nude. Pia was clearly in the throes of passion, encouraging the slant of Angelo's mouth over hers with reaching fingers while her ring caught the sunlight.

"The one with my hand on your shoulder is more elegant, don't you think?"

"For the eighteen hundreds, sure," Angelo mocked.

"I adore this," Melodie said of the kiss. "You

look like one of those timeless cinema couples from a classic black-and-white film."

"Keep the color," Angelo said, and insisted Melodie transfer it to him immediately, without working any editing magic. Within minutes, he had forwarded the photo to his publicity company.

Twenty minutes later, Pia's phone was making more noise than a popcorn popper. Colleagues, acquaintances, former students and fellow scientists wished her well. Social invitations began pouring in from every corner in ill-disguised attempts to be invited to the wedding.

She didn't have much chance to respond. The wedding planner arrived and details were decided on the fly because, according to Angelo, "We want to marry within the month."

Pia did prefer to marry before her pregnancy began to show, which gave them until mid-January. They wouldn't announce she was expecting until after the three-month scan, but her head whirled at the scale of wedding Angelo wanted in less than four weeks.

"A thousand?" Pia snapped her head around

when he said it. "Mother's assistant said five hundred."

"That was her estimate for how many she would invite. I'll have the same."

A thousand people. They might as well be televising the event while performing it naked on a beach.

She reminded herself that the half dozen pairs of eyes in his lounge this afternoon had been excruciating. It could be *ten* thousand at this point and it would be the same torture.

As the day pressed on, she did what she always did when the spotlight turned on her and scorched her to the center of her soul. She focused on creating order and maintaining her posture and manners. She spoke in a clear voice and approached everything with a rational, objective view.

She also pretended this wasn't *her* wedding. It was one of her mother's galas that needed an appropriate theme for decor and menu. She didn't let herself care whether her bouquet was roses or calla lilies because if she concerned herself with small details, she would work herself into a panic attack over the fact she would eventually have to stand in front of *a thousand people* and reveal that Angelo could make her knees weak simply by looking into her eyes.

Finally, Angelo dismissed everyone.

Exhausted, Pia made a point of shaking hands and saying goodbye to each person, then told Angelo flatly, "I'm going to change."

She needed to regroup.

Angelo couldn't believe what an ice queen he was marrying.

He should probably be grateful she had shut down somewhere between the stylist and the engagement ring. When he'd looked up as she entered, he'd been kicked in the stomach by how genuinely lovely she was. Speechless. Close to stammering.

She had walked across the room with such a standoffish expression, however, he'd become freshly annoyed. Insulted, even. She acted as though everyone around her was here to serve her and not worth a sincere smile or a personal word.

At least she liked the ring he had chosen, which had leaped out at him as somehow perfect. Subtle, yet with glints of fire. Mesmerizing and more complex the longer he stared at it.

Kissing her had been an impulse. A power move, maybe. He had wanted to force the thaw, and he had, but she'd nearly burned up any thought in his head except a desire to take her back to bed. Hell, if they hadn't been surrounded, he would have had her on the dining table.

Melodie's voice had yanked him back to reality.

Just as quickly, Pia had put on her lady-of-the-manor act and things had deteriorated from there. The photo shoot had turned into a parody of old sepia photos and when the eager-to-please wedding planner had invited Pia to describe her dream wedding, she had pretty much recoiled.

"Stay with tradition wherever possible. Many of these decisions can be fielded by my mother's personal assistant."

Her mother's *assistant*. Apparently, Angelo *was* being swapped into position like an outfielder midgame. If things were different, that would give him pause as to whether he wanted to marry her, but they had a baby on the way. He went ahead with the announcement.

Which prompted hundreds of texts and emails.

He left many of those to his own assistant, but sent a quick note to his team, reassuring them nothing would change and promising to speak to them soon.

Pia might answer to her parents and their staid ideas of tradition, but Angelo had his team of gamers, misfits all of them, but who were as genuine and generous as the ones who had taken him in so many years ago. They earned disgusting amounts of money, but they were kids and they had been knocked off guard by his news. Angelo paid back his karma by looking after them as best he could.

If he had thought Pia would provide a maternal influence for them, he would be sorely disappointed. She was so freaking detached. That remark about guests, for instance. Maybe she knew he was being perverse, determined to invite as many guests as her mother, down to the exact number. Even so, she was acting as though she was planning a funeral, not their wedding.

She faltered as she realized he was following her into the bedroom.

"I want to change, too. I hate suits." He didn't hate them that much now that he could afford them and had them tailored to fit like a second skin.

"Try heels," she muttered, and turned her back, gathering her hair to offer her zipper.

He almost asked if that was what had put such a sour look on her face, but as he lowered the zip, he revealed the black lace beneath.

"Strapless. I wondered what you were wearing." He traced the band of the bra to the hook and eye closure.

She moved away, into the closet. He toed off his shoes and opened his belt, tugging it free as he followed her.

She was buttoning one of his black shirts over her delightfully pretty black underwear, shoes abandoned beside the dress on the floor.

"May I?" she belatedly asked, rolling a sleeve up her delicate wrist.

"Hell, yes, you may." He eyed her legs. "I may refuse to buy you any clothes of your own." He meant it.

"I'll buy them myself." She walked out of the closet.

He bit back a curse.

"Stop playing mind games. If you're angry, say so. I won't chase you around this house begging you to tell me what's wrong."

"I'm not angry." She came back into the closet, brushing by him in the doorway. "I don't even know how to play mind games." She yanked open a drawer, slammed it, opened another.

"What, then? Why are you acting like I've got a gun to your head? Are you really that embarrassed to marry me?"

"I never said that." She paused, seeming genuinely surprised, but still cross. Her color was high.

"You're treating our wedding planner the way I treat my doctor when he tells me to turn my head and cough."

"I was perfectly civil!" she cried with a complete lack of civility. She went back to slamming through drawers. "I don't like being the center of attention. I hate it. Loathe it. There are no words ugly enough for how much I despise being stared at. The fact that you're standing there watching me melt down because I can't find my pants is my own personal nightmare and I hate myself for being this way, but I *am*."

She stopped, eyes welling, cheeks flushed, arms folded over her shuddering breasts.

Angelo reached out and dragged her jeans off a hanger where they hung in plain sight at eye level. "See, if you had asked my thoughtful and efficient staff..."

She grabbed them and shoved her legs into them, giving a little hop to snug her bottom into the seat. She might have sniffed, but it could have been the sound of the zip.

"I hated the idea of a big wedding when I thought I'd be marrying someone *normal*. Someone unremarkable. Like me." She gathered up the tails of the shirt and knotted them with shaking hands. "I *want* a hole-and-corner wedding and photos that are so boring no one even looks at them. I don't want photos that make me look like—"

She started to brush by him but he leaned to block the doorway, one shoulder against the casing, arms folded, trapping her into continuing this conversation.

"Like what?"

She hugged herself, brow crinkled. "Like I feel," she admitted in a strained voice.

The house could have exploded and he would have stayed in this timeless bubble with her, every word ringing with impact.

"How do you feel?" he asked.

"I don't know! I've never been allowed to feel, have I?" She flicked at her hair so it wasn't in her eyes. "Like my toddler nephew. Confused. Irrational. Like I should be able to make sense of this. Make order from the chaos, but I don't have any control over what's happening to me or how I feel about it. I don't like being—"

"Human?" he suggested dryly.

"It's never been encouraged," she said flatly. "You saw what they're like."

Her parents were definitely part of the problem, not the solution, but it was more than that. He saw the real issue now and wondered how he hadn't seen it sooner. The way she fell back on what she knew when her confidence flagged, how she used her big words to distance people and kept that aloof smile on her face. She was exactly like almost every gaming nerd he'd ever met—introverted and quiet and preferring to live in an alternate universe because participating in the real world was such a burden for her.

"You're shy," he accused.

She took a breath as though his words had struck somewhere tender.

"I am," she admitted miserably. "I always have been. Literally painfully shy. I feel the hurt inside me when people look at me. I hate that I have to work so hard to be as confident as…" She waved. "As all those people out there who talk like old friends when they've only met each other today."

"And right now? With me?"

"Like I have a pin in me, right here." She pointed to her chest. "Like there's a knife twisting, making each breath burn." She clenched her eyes shut, blinking at the ceiling to fight back her tears. "I wasn't supposed to have *any* feelings, especially bad ones. I certainly wasn't supposed to blush and cry and hide. I was supposed to get over it. Become a society maven who holds court over the masses the way my mother does. A fashion icon. A belle of the ball. Instead, it's a good thing she's incapable of disappointment because I am her greatest achievement in that regard."

"That's a lot of self-hatred. Maybe lighten up on yourself."

"I can't! You just accused me of treating the wedding planner like a molester. You told me to act like a human. Like I'm some kind of robot. I know I'm bad at this, Angelo. I've tried to learn how to get past it. Nothing works." She scowled, but he saw the flex of anguish beneath.

"Is that why you bury yourself in research?"

"Tried to, but girls aren't allowed to like science in my family," she grumbled. "I hated dresses until my brother told me about silkworms, then it gave me something interesting to think about when I had to wear one. And yes, pursuing my doctorate made for a convenient argument against being rushed into marriage. It was a great excuse to avoid a lot of mindless socializing, but I like it, too."

"You really are as efficient as you are intelligent." He wasn't being sarcastic. He was impressed. He had street smarts that wouldn't quit, but academically he'd been more of a skater, capable of better grades, but only finishing the American high school equivalency at night school when he was in his early twenties. Even then, he had only done as much work as necessary to pass.

"It's also the only way I've ever been able to connect meaningfully with my family. My father especially, but my brothers, as well. I've always been a detriment on a social level, but I held up the Montero reputation in scholarly circles. Advanced it even, which my mother appreciates. To a point."

"Does your father?"

She didn't say anything. After a moment, she

sighed. "My father isn't equipped to appreciate gestures. I wonder sometimes if he felt like I did as a child, or if he's on a spectrum of some kind. He's a genius and he genuinely doesn't care about social niceties. Somewhere along the line, he concluded very logically that a lack of diplomacy would hold him back so he married my mother to take care of that for him. She never talks about her childhood. I only know there was a title and little else, which means she holds very tightly to the life they've built together."

"And sacrificing her daughter in order to maintain that life is justified?" He clenched his teeth with repulsion.

"She doesn't see it that way. She thinks she was finding me the sort of partner she has, one who has worked with her to build a life that benefits all of us. I'm part of that team, Angelo. I had one job—to reset the family reputation. And I completely fell apart. The worst part is, all this distress and guilt I'm wallowing in? Completely useless. They don't care that I feel sick about it. *They're* not happy or sad or anxious or furious. They're *inconvenienced.*" She flung out a hand, trembling all over. "They'll get over it while I'll live the rest of my life with this grating knowledge that I let them down. Now you want me to be some sort of princess bride and I'm going to fail at that, too."

"No, you won't. Come here." He had to hold her, she was shaking so badly. He moved into the closet and gathered her into his arms, cradling her against his chest, soothing her trembling body with a gentle massage of her back and petting her silky hair. "Cry if you need to."

She rubbed her face into his chest as she shook her head. "I never cry."

Because she wasn't allowed to? Hell, he had shed a tear the first time he'd had four figures in his bank account. Last night, as he had held her soft, naked body against him, he'd let his hand rest on her stomach and his throat had closed up. His chest was tight listening to her struggle right now.

She held on to him at least, trusting and

warm, letting him rub her spine and try to comfort her.

"I won't make you be something you're not. I promise you," he said into her hair.

"But that's the problem," she groaned. "I *agree* with you. I don't want our baby to look back and think I was embarrassed. I want him or her to feel loved."

He drew in a sharp breath, stunned by how deeply her words pierced his heart. His lips against her hair turned into a kiss of gratitude.

"Thank you for that," he said, profoundly moved. "I was treated like blasphemy. Sent to boarding school so I wouldn't be seen or heard. I *need* this baby to be welcomed and accepted."

"I do, too." She lifted her face, mouth quivering. "I mean, beneath all the angst of planning a wedding and photos and distress at how my parents reacted, I'm really excited." She blinked matted lashes. "Insanely excited."

"Me, too." He cupped her jaw, such tenderness welling in him that he could hardly breathe.

She melted into him and he had to let his mouth settle over her unsteady smile.

Her clothes quickly wound up on the floor next to his, but she didn't seem to mind having to search again later.

CHAPTER EIGHT

THEIR PHOTO WENT VIRAL.

"I don't understand," Pia said, trying not to have heart palpitations two days later as they were traveling back to Valencia. "How are we still trending? Are you *that* famous?"

"In the gaming community, I'm afraid so," he said dryly.

"Because of your chip? My father invented one of the first lightweight, scratch-resistant metals for laptops. No one is excited in *that* community."

"Before our chip, I was one of the public faces in gaming, promoting championships and color commentating."

"I read that in your bio when I first looked you up." She frowned, still confused by this. "You really run tournaments like any other sport industry? Why would people enjoy watching other people play video games?"

"The same reason people who play beer league football also like to watch the World Cup. They follow players' careers and enjoy watching great plays by their favorite teams. They root for them to win."

She shook her head. "I don't follow sports. I may never fully comprehend that mindset. Why are your fans so suspicious of my motives?" *Gold digger. Outsider.* She threw her phone down. "Are you a gamer? How did you become involved in it?"

"Chance." He set aside his own phone as their flight attendant brought their breakfast. "I stumbled into one of the early e-sport tournaments by answering an ad to help move equipment. I connected with a player who had flown in from America to work the event hoping to find a sponsor, but he was terrible at networking. Didn't like to take the initiative. I got us a meeting that wasn't successful, but it went well enough that when he heard I was homeless, he offered his sofa if I could get myself to LA. His house should have been condemned, but I worked on a freighter for a month, then worked under the table to help with rent. On my days off, I figured out how the promotion side of gaming works. When you're hungry, you hustle. I was starving."

She blinked. "Why were you homeless? Was this after you left boarding school?"

His face blanked, perhaps regretting he had shared so much. "My tuition was halted when I was fourteen."

"Why?"

"My mother died. My father's family no longer saw a need to maintain my upkeep."

"And cut you off at *fourteen*?" Her teen years had been agonizing and lonely, but at least she'd had a roof over her head.

She glanced at her phone where other comments had ranged from comparing her to a scantily clad female ninja character in a particular game to questioning whether she "deserved" to become part of Angelo's beloved team.

"No wonder they idolize you for what you've made of yourself. You're very inspirational."

"In an industry of introverts, an extrovert is king," he drawled. "I'm inviting my team to our engagement party. They'll hate it as much as you will."

"I won't hate it," she protested, even though she already hated it a little, mostly because it had ruffled so many feathers.

Angelo was fixated on having their party tonight, but her parents had already been committed to another function elsewhere. It would be bad form for La Reina not only to back out, but to host a competing event, even if it was for her daughter. Angelo had booked it at his hotel and suggested her parents come by when time allowed.

That had still left her mother in the position of backing out of their own social event because they couldn't possibly be anywhere but at their daughter's engagement. Pia had tried shifting Angelo on the date, but he'd been adamant. At the last moment, Cesar and Sorcha had swooped in to insist they host the party at their home. It was a strategy straight from the Montero playbook, taking back home court advantage.

Pia's parents had had to withdraw from the other affair, something at which her father was supposed to have presented an award. That was bad enough, but they weren't the only ones jumping ship in favor of the far more exclusive event up the coast. If anyone held more social sway in the country than La Reina Montero, it was her son's wife, Sorcha. Dignitaries attended for the chance to rub shoulders with the Duque and Duquessa, while young professionals, jet-setters and the fashionably elite wouldn't miss a chance to mingle with the Montero heir.

Pia had quit reading her texts. She didn't know who she was causing to be snubbed and didn't care, too busy with her own concerns. Along with the multitude of calls and emails with her own accountant and the family lawyers and PR team, she was working with her stylist to curate her wardrobe for the events they faced through the holiday season and into her wedding in mid-January. She was trying to be nicer to the wedding planner, but the young woman was underfoot at every turn with questions and samples and suggestions.

Finding a wedding dress on short notice had meant calling in a favor with a friend of Sorcha's in Italy. Her poor designer had had to swear a blood oath to keep Pia's pregnancy under wraps until such time as they wanted to announce it, and Pia still hadn't settled on a dress for tonight.

Then there was the act of moving from the gorgeous little house her maternal aunt had bequeathed to her to the island mansion where an interior designer was already asking about nursery furniture.

"Of course you should keep this house if you want to," Angelo said as he wandered the rooms of her home, taking in the earthy tones and comfortable furniture. "It will give us our own space when we come to visit your family. You'll have to convert one of these rooms to a nursery, though."

"Oh dear Lord," Pia whimpered.

Angelo chuckled as he kissed her forehead. "Why don't you nap before we have to dress and leave for your brother's?"

"I have so much to do." She could barely face it, though.

"I'll wake you before I leave for my meeting," he promised, nudging her into the bedroom, where he draped a blanket over her.

She should have known he was lying.

Two hours later, the jangle of the landline woke her. Few people used it beyond her family or the occasional call from the grocer. She answered in time to hear her housekeeper on the extension telling the caller she wasn't available and offer to take a message.

"I'm here," Pia said. "Who's calling?"

"This is Tomas Gomez, Señorita Montero. Do you know who I am?"

"I'll take it," Pia said, sitting up. The phone clicked as her housekeeper hung up. "I believe my brother Rico now owns an estate that previously belonged to your family."

"That's right. It was in our family for generations. Do you know why Angelo was on the estate the night of the masked ball?"

"W-was he?" She instinctively played dumb, mostly because she was so surprised to receive this call.

"He was there for more than the painting, Pia. But you already know that, don't you? Were you helping him?"

Her skin crawled at his use of her name, but she couldn't seem to hang up the phone. "In what way? I don't know what you're talking about."

"The jewelry. Did you help him retrieve it?"

She caught her breath loudly enough he must have heard it.

"Where is it? Can you get it?"

"It's in the possession of a security company." She said it out of instinctive fear he would break in here looking for the treasure if she wasn't frank about it. "Why are you talking to me about this, rather than Angelo?"

"Don't you want to know that your fiancé is a thief? A con artist? It's no accident he booked your engagement party for the night your parents were scheduled to attend an event where *I* will receive some well-deserved recognition for my philanthropy. That's what kind of man he is. He's trying to buy respectability by attaching himself to you while nursing an old grudge against people he knows are better than he is. Your mother would be horrified if she knew the truth of his background.

Not that I'll say anything. If you can get me the jewels?"

She shuddered at his sly tone. Tomas was no better than the kind of man he was describing. She distantly heard the front door.

"He's coming." She hung up.

Her skin was clammy, her mind whirling. Had Angelo known who she was that night? Had he followed her to the rooftop and purposely seduced her to put her in this position of having to marry him? Why had he been there? For the painting, yes, but something else? Something on the rooftop? A tin full of jewelry, perhaps?

The door opened and her intended entered. His charming, *"Querida,"* rang falsely. "What's wrong?" He frowned.

"You said you would wake me," she mumbled, not having to pretend a scattered mind as she rose, head aching and spinning. "I need to get ready."

Despite her aversion to shining brightly, Pia wore a silver dress covered in tinsel-like beadwork. It scooped across the tops of her breasts and ended midthigh. Her feet were in some sort of glass slippers that completed the icicle look.

He smiled darkly in the back of the car, beginning to enjoy the private knowledge that he alone knew how easily she melted under his kiss or caress.

"We have time," he pointed out, glancing at the closed privacy screen.

It was an hour to her brother's villa and, he discovered to his consternation, he longed quite badly to touch her. This afternoon's meeting with her brothers had been tense, their contempt for him undisguised. He ached to fill his hands with her, catch her cries of pleasure in his mouth and reaffirm that she belonged to him. She'd seemed befuddled and distracted when he arrived home, but now...

"Come here," he invited.

"I had a call while you were out," she said in a hollow voice. "From Tomas Gomez. He asked about the jewelry."

For a wallflower, she excelled at delivering a surprise crosscut that snapped a jaw. A nest of snakes came alive in his belly.

"What did you tell him?"

"That you left them with a security company. That's what Melodie's husband is, isn't he? A security expert?"

Top in his field, globally.

"So you confirmed to Tomas that I had the jewels." A call to Pia had been inevitable, he supposed. The scumbags wouldn't confront *him* if they could unsettle a woman or turn her against him.

"He asked if I helped you retrieve them," she continued in that empty voice. "Did I?"

A metallic taste filled his mouth. "Inadvertently," he admitted.

"On the rooftop." Her voice developed a pang that made him feel as though she was slipping through his fingers. "That's why you seduced me."

"Our lovemaking just happened, Pia."

"Did it? He said you're using me to climb society's ladder. You knew who I was!"

"I have my own society. I don't need yours," he spat, even as panic dug talons into him. "Don't listen to that piece of garbage. He's a liar." *Don't side with him.*

"He called *you* a liar. And a thief."

"It takes one to know one," he muttered. White-hot anger grew into a spiked ball inside him, too painful to contain. "But I've never lied to you."

"Only hidden the truth."

"Do you *want* the truth?"

"I don't know. Will it make me an accessory to whatever crimes you've committed? My brother bought the Gomez villa *and its contents*. If you took something more than the painting you purchased, you were stealing."

"I didn't steal anything. I retrieved something my mother left for me. I retrieved my *mother*."

She snapped her head around to look at him. "Not the girl in the painting. She's too young."

"Her name is Angelica. It's the only image I have of her. She was the daughter of the baron's second wife from her first marriage and yes, she was far too young to be a mother. *My* mother." Despite a lifetime of damming up the truth behind shame and anger, the toxic words spilled out of him in a torrent. "The accusation is that she took the jewelry from her mother's bedroom," he said, his voice low and gritty and brimming with three decades of helpless hatred. "I am quite certain it was all brought to her by my father, since it was kept in the safe in his office. He spent time with my mother when his wife, my grandmother, had gone out for the day."

Pia covered her mouth, eyes wide with horror.

"I suppose I'm lucky I wasn't thrown into a river or given away when she had me. At *fifteen*. I had six years with her in that moldy little cottage before they sent me to that prison they called a boarding school. I barely saw her after that. Don't ask me why she stayed. To ensure my tuition was paid, I imagine. Maybe she felt too damned fragile to fight for a better life. All I know is that she killed herself shortly after my father died, well aware she would be turned onto the street otherwise. *I* was."

Angelo's acrid fury clouded the darkened back seat of the car.

Pia was speechless, utterly unable to form thoughts into words she was so anguished on his mother's behalf. Pia was overwhelmed and frightened by her pregnancy and she was an adult with resources. She had a support system and her baby's father was beside her in this journey, putting her down for naps when she was too overtired to see the sense in it.

"Did your grandmother know?" she managed to gasp.

"Of course she did. Everyone in the family knew. They also knew which side their bread was buttered on, so they let it go on."

"That's horrific." She couldn't grasp it. It was too awful.

"It is. And if my half brothers want the jewels back, they can damned well acknowledge how my mother came by them, not call my future wife and tell her I *stole* them. They can admit I'm as entitled as they are to a share in the family fortune."

"But you could... I mean, wouldn't a DNA test—"

"I could insist on a test," he said, cutting her off with a biting tone. "This isn't about proving our relationship any more than it is about the money. I hate that I carry any trace of their tainted blood. They can have the damned name and title. Protecting that is why her *own mother* allowed her to be abused. No, I'm quite content to remain an ugly family secret, but I won't let them continue to enjoy the life they lead when it came at her expense. I'm taking it apart brick by brick."

"Why can't you…?" She balked even as she started to say it.

"Tell the world what happened? Put my mother on trial in the court of public opinion? My brothers will claim she instigated what happened to her. That's what kind of people they are. My poor, upstanding, blameless father, a grown man, was helpless against a teenage seductress. Who are *your* parents going to believe, Pia? The bastard with a grudge? Or one of their own?"

They would distance themselves as much as possible, she suspected. Her entire body went cold.

"I wish you had told me sooner," she said, projecting to the ramifications if this came out.

"When?" he demanded. "While we were two strangers having our tête-à-tête on the rooftop? When you were informing me that we'd conceived a child? Or do you mean before we publicly attached ourselves with the engagement photo? Frightened to be associated with me now, Pia?"

She looked guiltily to the window, heart clenching at his scathing tone.

"There's still time to back out." His gritty voice dared her to try. "I'll make it very uncomfortable for you if you do."

She glanced back to see him sitting with his clenched fists on his thighs, his profile cast in iron. How comfortable would he make it for her to continue forward and marry him, she wondered hysterically? Especially if the truth came out?

There might as well have been a wall of ice between them the rest of the drive. She didn't know how to reach past it and wasn't sure she wanted to. When he had asked her to trust him that first night, she hadn't expected anything of this magnitude. She felt tricked, especially when he was speaking so ruthlessly about going through with their marriage. He was hardly motivated by any genuine feeling toward her, was he?

Her angst made her smile all the more strained when they arrived at Cesar's mansion to find Rico and Poppy were already there along with her parents. The rest of the guests weren't due for an hour, but Sorcha had wanted a chance to break the ice and get to know Angelo.

"Pia, would you be a love and pop up to say good-night to the boys?" Sorcha entreated while she was removing her coat. "Enrique found a shell the other day. He's convinced you're the only one who can identify it." She took hold of Angelo's arm. "You, however, look like a man who might be up for sampling my stock of Irish whiskey. Can I tempt you?"

Pia was dying for a moment to collect her thoughts and the children always restored her. "I'll join you shortly," she promised Angelo, and veered up the stairs.

She had only been with her nephews for five short minutes, however, when Cesar came in.

"Tía is expected downstairs," he told the

boys in a gentle but firm voice, his affectionate stroke of his older son's hair softening the
blow.

"We'll have a proper visit soon," she promised them.

"Christmas," Enrique whispered with a grin
of anticipation.

"Exactly." Pia couldn't help cupping his little face and kissing his forehead. She did the
same to Mateo and blew another kiss at them
as she left.

Cesar stopped her turning down the hall toward the stairs, opening the door to the play-
room across the hall and waving her in with
an imperious look.

"Oh, I see. It wasn't the boys who wanted
to see me." Why was that such a kick in the
chest?

"They always want to see you, but so did I."
Cesar swung the door mostly closed.

Pia crossed a loomed mat imprinted with a
town of roadways and buildings, stopped at
the indoor slide and turned to face her brother,
arms folded. Defensive? Absolutely. It was
bad enough she hadn't brought home some-

one from the preapproved list of bachelors. Her groom's backstory was even more shocking than any of them imagined and she was pregnant by him. Which meant she'd had *sex*.

It didn't matter that Cesar had been in this position himself. His role had been the other side and he'd never been as sensitive about having his private business strewn about, probably because he was secure in his place in the family and the world.

What made this confrontation particularly difficult, however, was the fact that she liked her brothers. Their marrying wonderful women had certainly helped her feel closer to them, but Cesar especially was the person she most hated to disappoint. He had suffered betrayals from other quarters and once his trust was lost, it was never regained.

She braced herself for his rebuke.

"You don't have to marry him," he said flatly. "Ignore whatever Mother has said about how things look. *I* will always look after you."

She was too shocked to react. They never spoke from the heart. The most sentimental thing he'd ever said to her was his sincere thanks for her presence at his wedding because it had meant so much to Sorcha.

This conversation instantly became uncomfortable. She reflexively pointed out the obvious. "I've been living independently for five years. I can take care of myself."

"Clearly," he said, which was a rebuke, but a gentle one.

"Lovely glass house you live in," she retorted.

"It is," he agreed, nodding with gravity. "Which is why I'm telling you to do what's right for *you*. I will back you up with Mother, support you in any and every way you need. How well do you even know this man, Pia?" Now he sounded like the clichéd big brother. "The gaps in his background report make me suspicious."

"You had him investigated?"

Cesar snorted. "If you think he doesn't have a hundred-page dossier on every single one of us, you really do need someone to start looking after you."

Maybe she did, because her first thought went to how badly it would hurt Angelo to have his mother's pain uncovered by some paid snoop, then subsequently held up as a blight on his character. That poor young girl had been in an untenable situation. She had given birth to a baby she shouldn't have conceived and loved him enough to protect and provide for him the only way she could. Pia's heart fractured thinking of her.

"His lawyers are sharks," Cesar continued. "Negotiations have been heated."

"*Our* lawyers are sharks," she dismissed. She'd been copied on everything and thought it was going as well as it could, given both sides had proprietary interests to protect.

"How long have you known him? Are you in love? Don't tie yourself to him because you think you have to. I want to hear it from *you* that this is what you want."

She parted her lips, but discovered it was only to draw in a deep sigh.

Still time to back out, she heard Angelo saying. Those words had hurt because he hadn't tried to convince her to stay with him. He had threatened to make her life difficult if she didn't. One more indication his desire to marry wasn't about her at all. No matter how great the sex, he was marrying her for the baby and possibly other, darker motives.

The irony was, his devotion to their child carried tremendous weight with her.

"He wants this baby, Cesar. In a way that—" She cut herself off, unwilling to go down the road of their father's shortcomings. There was no point.

Cesar got there anyway. "That's why you have to do what's right for you," he said gently. "I didn't have the power to make things better for you when we were young. I do now. *You* do. Say the word and I will end this engagement right now."

What could she say? That she *wanted* to marry a man who had stolen something that technically belonged to Rico? That she wanted a husband whose history could come to light and throw a shadow over all of them? That she hoped whatever scandal arose, it would blow over before their child was old enough to understand any of it and would never be harmed by it?

"Pia?" he prompted.

"Tell me something, Cesar." She had to clear the huskiness from her throat before she continued. "Do you blame Sorcha for the fact her father had two families? That she was part of the illegitimate one?"

"Of course not," he snapped. "Her father's behavior had nothing to do with her."

"Will you please remember that if anyone talks to you about Angelo?"

"What are you saying? Forewarned is forearmed. Tell me everything."

"It's not mine to tell," she said as the door swung inward, silent on its hinges.

Angelo stood there, one shoulder negligently braced against the jamb.

She knew immediately he'd been there long enough to hear her comparison of his circumstance to Sorcha's, maybe more.

Keeping his gaze locked with Pia's, he said to Cesar, "Your wife does not have a promising career on the magician's circuit. Her attempt at misdirection was blatant and obvious." He held out his hand to Pia. "She is, however, an extremely charming hostess. I don't wish to be rude. Shall we rejoin our party, *querida*?"

She knew her acquiescence would be agreement to more than a party. The engagement would proceed. The wedding would happen. Chips would fall as they may.

Cesar was wrong. She didn't have the power here. Her baby did. And she genuinely believed Angelo would love their child. Maybe some hidden part of her even saw that as potential he might one day love *her*.

She moved to set her hand in his and they went back downstairs.

CHAPTER NINE

THEIR ENGAGEMENT EVENING went quite well, all things considered. Angelo hadn't meant to tell Pia the truth so baldly, driving it between them like a wedge. Maybe he'd had to do it with anger in order to get it out and brace himself for what he expected would be a rejection.

Her family's maneuverings, allowing her to slip away for an intervention from big brother, hadn't surprised him one bit. He had accepted a whiskey and told himself he would be better off if she broke their engagement. He had no desire to become part of this stuck-up family and suffer their judgment for the rest of his life. He didn't want to stare into her eyes across the breakfast table every morning and see—

With a choke, he'd set aside his drink and

went looking for her, leaving a surprised pause behind him.

He had arrived at the cracked door in time to hear her brother's script spoken exactly on cue. Pia quite easily could have spilled everything Angelo had revealed to protect her own family from future scandal, but she hadn't. She had shielded his mother in the only way she could, by maintaining her privacy.

That kindness nearly broke him. He had kept her hand in his the rest of the night, doing everything he could to ease her tension as they made the rounds with guests. When they made love that night, it had been with something new between them—the first strands of trust.

But it was immediately put to the test.

Now that Tomas and Darius knew Angelo had the jewels, their campaign to discredit him began in earnest. Rumormongering online suggested everything from accusations of child labor to tax evasion. Paparazzi began tailing them and a woman he'd never met claimed to be pregnant with his child.

Angelo took sensible steps. He had Pia's housekeeper change the phone number and instructed her staff to screen all communications. His security team upgraded the alarm system on her house, a pair of guards began to shadow them when they went out, and another pair remotely monitored for suspicious activity.

None of that could protect them from the whispers and snide asides that followed them into cocktail parties and benefits. Much of the animosity was pure snobbery couched as concern for Pia.

"He's American, isn't he?" he overheard a woman ask Pia in an outraged whisper, because *that* was a crime.

"Spanish," Pia said evenly. "America is where his head office is located. He has a home in California."

"Are you moving there? Because if he isn't part of *this* life, how will he fit in? I mean, have an affair. *Look* at him. But I can't see you *marrying* him."

"Is that a regret for the wedding? I'll let Mother know."

The woman's face had dropped and Angelo had seized the opportunity to draw Pia onto the dance floor, taking dark satisfaction in giving the woman no time to rephrase after Pia's cutthroat response.

Pia's mother was concerned that RSVPs weren't coming in thick and fast, though. It was another indicator that people were dragging their feet as they debated taking sides. So far, Angelo wasn't winning.

Pia wasn't winning, either. He'd thrust her smack in the middle of his war. Perhaps that should have prompted an apology from him, but he was so disgusted by her crowd's desire to turn on what they perceived to be an outsider, he could only bite out, "Hypocrites."

They had just arrived at a hotel ballroom to be informed by a greeter they weren't on the list.

Angelo's brothers were keeping a low profile, probably not even here, but that was what made this worse. They were getting the word out that Angelo was *persona non grata* and it was working.

"This is exactly what happened to my mother," Angelo said as they stepped away from the entrance to a nearby alcove. "Any friends she might have made in her early years disappeared, not standing by her at all. They preferred to suck onto my father like lampreys and continue to benefit from his influence. They're still doing it. How can you want to be counted among these blue-blooded parasites?"

"I don't," Pia said stiffly. "You know my feelings on parties. These weeks of making appearances, providing nothing but fodder for gossip, have been hell. I'm here for *you*."

"For your parents, you mean," he shot back. "And your father's delicate reputation."

"If you and I slink off, never to be seen or heard from again, my parents will be better than fine. My mother would prefer our notoriety die a quick and permanent death. No, I'm dragging myself through all of this for you. I don't agree with your methods, but I do agree that people are backing the wrong horse. Even more, this is about how our child will be accepted in the future. That starts with us staking our right to be here now."

She had pulled out her phone and was scrolling through her contacts as they spoke. She tapped out a text, throwing her phone back into her clutch.

"Who was that?"

"Someone who had better remember the numerous alibis her cerebral roommate provided in a desperate effort to fit in."

"To hell with that." Her words about their child had struck home. He took her hand and glared down the greeter as he drew Pia into the party. If this crowd thought they could ostracize him, they could try saying it to his face.

Inside, the decor marked the year change with balloons and streamers. Champagne cascaded down a pyramid of glasses. Hundreds of vintage clocks littered the ballroom, meant to be taken home as swag. A chanteuse presided over a dance floor, crooning a modern pop tune, but she was barely audible over the din of convivial guests.

The chattering voices slowly petered off as heads turned to stare, leaving the breathy singer sounding overloud. She was a professional, however, and didn't miss a beat as she transitioned into a rendition of something from a film soundtrack.

Pia, however, wasn't as unaffected. She dug her nails into the back of his hand.

Angelo was genuinely sorry to put her on the spot this way, but he would be damned if he would back out now.

"As usual, *mi sirenita*, your beauty is turning heads." He lifted her hand to kiss her knuckles.

In the last few weeks, she had begun embracing bolder colors and styles. Tonight, she was stunning in an aqua gown with a mermaid skirt that inspired his endearment.

Predictably, a composed Mona Lisa smile was her only response.

"You have a nerve," a man said, weaving forward through the crowd.

Darius. Angelo recognized him with a lurch in his chest. Drunk and mean, as usual.

Angelo felt both sickened and murderous. He was fourteen and helpless again, yet mature and powerful and cold-bloodedly willing to fight this man to the death.

He instinctively tried to draw Pia behind him, but she set her cool hand over his knuckles and wiggled her fingers, drawing his attention to the fact he was crushing her hand in his grip. His lungs burned and he would have shoved forward to confront Darius, but a scantily clad redhead emerged from the crowd.

"Pia!" She waved off the security guard who had been about to put his hand on Angelo's shoulder. There really would have been bloodshed if he'd managed it.

"I'm so glad you could come!" The woman air-kissed Pia's pale cheeks. "You all know Pia Montero," she announced to the crowd at large. "One of my dearest friends from my misspent youth. Don't say a *word* about our exploits," she warned Pia with a girlish laugh. "And this is your infamous fiancé." She batted her lashes at Angelo. "We've been hearing *so* much about you. Please let me introduce you around."

As hideous evenings went, this one took the prize, but Pia recognized a turning point when she stood on one, mostly because it twisted her stomach into knots.

This had been the most blatant attempt to snub them yet, and she'd had to gather every shred of courage she possessed to tackle it. She had hated leaning on one of the very connections Angelo found so contemptuous, but it had *worked*. Much to her astonishment. She rarely reached out to any of her acquaintances, especially young women from boarding school. They might as well have been a different species, she'd had so little in common with them.

But along with understanding how difficult it would be to come back from any sort of retreat, she had wanted to make Angelo see that not everything in her family's titled life was a false front for dark acts. Maybe this wasn't "their" type of people, but that didn't make every single person here a terrible one.

Of course, there were definitely some awful examples, she noted with an inward groan as a drunk staggered up and poked his finger into Angelo's ruffled tuxedo shirt.

"You—"

Angelo grabbed the man's hand in what looked like a warm, thumb-grabbing handshake that drew the man in close. Only Pia saw that he squeezed tightly enough his knuckles went white and so did the man's face. Angelo used his other hand to grip the man's bent arm. His thumb dug into the soft flesh above his elbow as he said, "Darius," through gritted teeth.

Dios mio. She saw the resemblance, but only vaguely. Any good looks Darius had once possessed had been sacrificed on the altar of poor life choices.

"Angelo," she murmured, affecting a calm smile as she glanced around.

Most people had lost interest in them now that they'd been introduced as the latest celebrity couple. A few stared unabashedly, though.

"You black sheep bastard. You knew where it was all along," Darius choked.

"I know where it is now. Shall I tell the auction house you'd like a catalog? So you can purchase what you've wanted to get your filthy hands on for so long? Proceeds will go to a charity for pregnant teenagers. A worthy cause you'll want to support, I'm sure."

Darius snorted dismissively only to stiffen and make a strangled noise, telling Pia that Angelo had exerted an extra pulse of pressure.

"I'm reporting this to the police," Darius

threatened, voice straining with agony. "Theft. Assault."

"You go right ahead," Angelo said, staring with dead eyes into his brother's. "You tell your story. I'll tell mine."

"You're proving what an animal you are."

"Keep pushing me, Darius. See what happens."

Sweat broke in beads on Darius's upper lip.

"You don't look well, *hermano*. Go home," Angelo advised in a voice that raised the hair on the back of Pia's neck. "Never let me see you again."

He released him and Darius staggered away.

Angelo gave his hands a quick wipe on his thighs.

Pia pasted on her most unruffled smile and took his hand, leading him onto the dance floor. It was the last thing she wanted to do. They were both stiff and uncoordinated as he took her in his arms. She felt the clash of his heart battering in his rib cage through the layers of their clothes. Her own heart was falling down a perpetual flight of stairs, but she hid it with a stock expression of serenity.

Concern for Angelo had her scanning his granite features. He was a million miles away, his mind in some dark place that prevented him from finding the beat in the music and dancing as smoothly as he usually did.

When it came to physical contact, she usually let him initiate it. She only ever felt comfortable touching him freely when they were in bed, naked and entwined, shields on the floor with their clothes.

She slid light fingers against the side of his neck, though, caressing to get his attention.

"It's a worthy cause," she said. "I didn't know that was what you were doing with the proceeds. I think any mother would be proud of a son who was doing everything he could to right such a wrong done to her. I'm very sorry I will never meet her."

"Me, too," he said, drawing her in tighter with a firm touch that crashed her into his taut frame. He was still gripped by rage.

She let her head settle onto his shoulder, wholly unfamiliar with trying to offer comfort, but she ignored the music and the lively people surrounding them. She slipped her arms around his waist and tried to radiate strength and acceptance. Tried to heal him in some small way.

After a few moments, his hold on her changed. His hands moved across her back, settling her more securely against him. The tension gripping him eased. His lips touched her temple.

"Thank you," he murmured.

She wasn't sure what she'd done, but she closed her eyes, pleased to have helped him in some small way, hoping with all her heart he was finding the closure he needed.

For the first time, they didn't make love when they came home. Granted, it was well past midnight. Pia barely bothered to remove her makeup, while Angelo insisted he needed a shower. She didn't remember him coming to bed. She fell asleep hard and fast, but they made love in the morning.

He rose so abruptly afterward, however, she was compelled to ask, "Is everything all right?"

"Of course." He stood there in all his naked

glory, the flush of their lovemaking fading on his chest. His abdominal muscles were stacked and tense, though, his jaw shadowed by midnight stubble, his gaze flinty. "Thank you for having my back last night. Every night, lately. I hadn't realized, but now I do."

"Of course. That's what marriage is for."

"Is it?" His inscrutable gaze didn't waver from hers, making her self-conscious.

"From what I can tell." Her shrug nearly caused the sheet to slip. She wasn't sure why she was hiding behind it, but she felt awfully insecure despite their scorching connection moments ago.

He seemed very far away. Distant and watchful and displeased.

"I've judged my parents' loveless marriage more harshly than it deserves, I think," she said pensively, reevaluating something she'd only ever seen as coldly practical and lacking in personal regard. "There's value in a dedicated partnership where you can trust in the other and lean on their strength. You can become more than the sum of the parts. That's a relationship worth pursuing, I think."

He snorted, incredibly intimidating as he drilled her with his unwavering gaze. "You're still willing to marry me?"

Her heart leaped in alarm. He wanted to back out? Because he'd achieved acceptance? He didn't want her after all?

"Knowing what a black sheep bastard I am?" he continued.

"Don't," she murmured, recoiling at the depth of angry hurt that coated his tone.

"How are *you* going to balance *that* out?" He sounded both appalled and tortured. "How will you compensate for it? You can't. And they may yet force it to light, Pia."

"I don't know how I'll react." She curled her fingers into the edge of the sheet, her toes into the mattress. "But it won't change my commitment to you and our marriage. Not if we're both faithful and sincerely trying to make a life together."

He didn't seem particularly appeased. His jaw pulsed as he ground his teeth, his brooding gaze cast into the middle distance.

"We don't have to discuss any of this unless it becomes necessary." It was a cowardly avoidance of a hard subject, but she was terrified that the tentative bond they'd formed was disintegrating. It wasn't strong enough to withstand hard examination.

His cheek ticked and he nodded once, jerkily, and went to dress.

She slipped into the shower. She could have invited him to join her and wished she had, but she didn't know how to extend herself that way. It felt weak to want to touch him when they'd just been physically close.

She was afraid of rejection—that was the real issue. It didn't help that Angelo remained withdrawn and she didn't know how to bridge that gap.

At least their New Year's Eve appearance clinched their position as the couple to support. Acceptances to their wedding poured in.

Pia couldn't say she was relieved exactly, but for the sake of everyone involved she was thankful they had overcome whatever hurdle Angelo's brothers had posed.

Which freed her up to panic about the new life upon which she was embarking.

Angelo had spent the last weeks making inroads into the society that should have been his by birthright. Now she would take her place next to him on his turf, a global stage focused on the technology sector. She would have to become what she had always felt would make her a square peg in a round hole—the wife of a powerful man.

Angelo willingly stayed in her home in Valencia while they rode out these turbulent weeks into their shotgun wedding, but after their honeymoon in Australia, he intended to take her to America until her third trimester reduced her ability to travel. They would return to Spain until the baby was born, after which he expected they would divide their time between a handful of his preferred homes.

Along with learning the ropes of motherhood, which Pia looked forward to, she would continue decorating his arm and joining him at networking events. She would have to begin entertaining. Host *functions*.

So even though Angelo frowned with concern when she reported the final number was nine hundred and fifty guests, and said, "It's only one day," she knew it wasn't. It was a daunting lifetime of feeling isolated in a crowd.

"What have you done in the past to cope?" he asked, seeing something in her expression that made him set aside the tablet he was working on.

"Mostly I ran away," she joked, trying to dismiss her character deficiency even though he wasn't teasing or mocking her for it.

"What do you mean?"

"Well, they were legitimate field studies, but I might have left early for them." She looked at her nails. "Or stayed longer than strictly necessary. Or collected data for other researchers."

For the first time in days, he seemed to relax as he tilted a look at her that was both empathetic and indulgent. "Would you feel more comfortable holding a clipboard than a bouquet? Because I'm open to it."

She wrinkled her nose. "I'll try imagining it while I'm walking down the aisle. Maybe it will help."

"What have you decided with regards to research?" He pulled his earbuds out completely and left them atop his tablet, giving her his full attention. That always disconcerted her, but made her insides squirm today when she was trying to hide how disheartened she felt at the life she faced.

"I don't know that I'll have time to pursue any." She set aside her own tablet and the calendar that was being synced to his. Eaten up and overwhelmed.

"Because of the baby?"

"And your work. I'm looking at all these events you have scheduled and now your assistant is asking if I want to take an active role in some of your charities. That's the sort of thing my mother always did and—"

"You are not your mother," he cut in. "There are only a handful of events where your presence is important to me. I'll mark them and the rest are up to you. My people have done all my organizing until this point and can continue to do so. Our baby won't be as accommodating, though," he said wryly.

"I know," she said on a little sigh. "Fieldwork is out for several years, so I might as well take on charity work."

"We'll travel with you." He shrugged.

She choked out a dismissive laugh.

He frowned. "I'll help as much as possible from day one, Pia. That's why I want us to be a family. I realize it won't be easy to carve out time in the beginning, but I don't expect you to sacrifice that brain of yours to my photo ops. Is there something you can work on in the short term that's more piecemeal and can be done from home?"

She hesitated, rather stunned by his attitude. "This is weird for me. I've always had to work really hard to justify *wanting* to study. Mother thought it was a waste of time since she expected me to live a role like hers once I was married. I made a strong case for at least getting my doctorate, but my father and brothers have always questioned my interest in biology. The family business is alloys so they thought I should follow in their footsteps. Even when I fund from my own pocket, some professor is always quick to weigh in on whether my pursuit has merit or tell me my time and money could be better spent elsewhere. It's exhausting."

"Do I need to put on a cardigan and throw a

research fund-raiser to get your idea approved? I can do that. I can talk just about anyone into just about anything."

She'd noticed. She told him things she'd never told anyone.

"I've been contributing some of my data to a pregnancy study," she admitted. "It's a surprisingly understudied area. Women are considered to be vulnerable in this state, physically and mentally." She dismissed that with a roll of her eyes. "Obviously, we're not a testing ground for new drugs, but there are a lot of things that aren't known. I've been thinking about how to structure a few studies of my own—"

"Done. What do you need?"

"More pregnant women?" she suggested tartly, suppressing an astonished chuckle that he was so quick and unquestioning in his support.

He came to take her chin in a light pinch. "I will proceed with caution on producing more of those. I'm discovering they can be quite a handful. If there was some decent data warning of the real danger they pose, we men might show some restraint in making them."

"Oh, good luck with that," she sputtered.

"You're right." His teeth flashed in a grin of humor. "As if we'll read when we could put our time to better use." He winked. His irises shone with the warmth of a summer sky and he was so blindingly handsome in that moment that she caught her breath and thought, *Oh.*

This was why they called it falling. Her head swam and her feet couldn't feel the floor. The world tilted and her heart flipped and wind rushed in her ears. When his mouth touched hers, such a soaring joy gripped her, she thought she would burst.

That lightness carried her into her wedding day, putting secretive smiles on her sisters-in-law's faces as they fussed around her with the rest of the bridal party. Her stylist kept going on about the romance of the day and how there was so much "love in the air."

They know, Pia thought, desperately trying to hide her tender new feelings because the sense of exposure was so intense. And she didn't know how Angelo felt. Was he growing to care for her, too? Or was his support of her all part of a play they were enacting for the benefit of their child?

She dearly wished for a moment of privacy to collect herself, but solitude was the only luxury this wedding didn't afford her. She had to hide her insecurities behind a calm smile as she was harnessed into her mikado silk A-line gown and took the weight of her veil, covered in thousands of seed pearls, as it was draped over her hair.

Pia wasn't convinced she was worthy of romantic love anyway. Sorcha and Poppy, yes. They were warm and outgoing, witty and quick to laugh. They were so easy to adore— it was no wonder Pia's staid brothers had fallen head over heels.

Pia didn't even know where to start in making herself emotionally appealing. Whatever good qualities she had cultivated had never swayed her parents toward words or demonstrations of love. Even loving friendships were built on confidences, something she found difficult because the things she valued had rarely been valued by others. Her niece and nephews loved her, which felt like a miracle, but Pia didn't let it go to her head. Such well-loved children were factories for the recycling of it, pouring out adoration for anyone who brought them a toy or took them into the garden for an hour.

As for Angelo, she had shared more with him than anyone in her life, quite possibly revealing as many reasons *not* to love her. Who wanted a wife who fought tears because her wedding day felt like too big an ordeal to face? One who would rather wear woolen socks and rubber rain gear than a gown worth a quarter million euros?

The moment arrived and her father appeared to escort her. He looked flawless and handsome and said a polite, "You look lovely."

Pia waited an extra, agonizing second, hoping for something… Maybe that clichéd remark that he didn't want to lose her? That he was proud of her? That he forgave her for getting pregnant and forcing this wedding to the wrong man?

"Are you ready?"

The urge to cry lurched harder in her throat.

Love was impossible to force; she *knew* that. She also knew that longing for it made the lack of it even more painful. She couldn't pin her dreams on Angelo falling for her. Couldn't do that to herself and continue to suffer this ache the rest of her life.

She swallowed back her tears and let her father guide her to the top of the aisle.

The music changed and the guests stood and turned to watch her procession. She wanted to cling to her father's arm, but forced herself to hold to the pace he set and smile and breathe.

Her gaze snagged on Angelo's as she moved toward him. His attention flickered to her bouquet and she could practically hear his voice in her head. *Nice clipboard.*

She wanted to laugh, then. Laugh and cry and run up to hug him. The rest of the congregation fell away and no one existed in this cavernous church but the two of them as she came to a halt before him.

She was lucky, so lucky, to have him. Lucky to have passion and a devoted father for her child. It was all she truly needed.

It would have to be, because it was all they had.

Their special day was paved with rice and rose petals, but Angelo felt like the fraud he was.

His first dalliance with Pia had been just that, a pleasurable encounter that had been as pure as something that earthy and erotic could be. It had been free of ulterior motives, at least.

Then, when her pregnancy pulled them into a forced engagement, he hadn't cared what sort of uproar his appearance in her life might cause. In fact, he had embraced making waves in her patrician pond.

He hadn't cared because he hadn't *cared*. Now he was realizing how much his presence in her life was costing her. The greater the stakes became, the more it bothered him. He sure as hell wouldn't have allowed Darius anywhere near her if he could have avoided it.

He kept trying to forget that night even as moments from it flashed into his memory—

the snubbing at the door, Darius's punishing truth that Angelo would never be anything but the ill-begotten bastard he was.

Pia's revelation that she was putting herself through this trial *for him*. Yes, their end goal was the best life for their child, but he could spirit her and their baby to America and skip all this nonsense if they had to. He'd been ready to quit Europe altogether that evening. He was neither beholden nor sentimentally attached to his birthplace. He lived on the island in the Med because the climate suited him.

Pia, antisocial science nerd that she was, had an inner badass, though. One who came to the fore when she decided she wanted something. She had kept him at the party until midnight when he would have happily left minutes after his confrontation with Darius. She had circulated with her hand tucked firmly into his, smoothing any lasting rough edges, cementing their position as a power couple well above whatever basement level of hell his brothers might have slithered back into.

Much as Angelo was loath to care about such a puerile victory, it meant something to him that Pia had refused to give up on getting it for him. He was still stunned. Moved.

But somehow, in the crashing of his old world into his new one, his shell of anger had been shaken, crumbling enough to expose the shame beneath. Shame that leaked into a bigger stain as he realized he was pulling an innocent—no, two innocents—into the mire of his origin story.

He had gone to bed that night convinced he should break things off with her. Of course, he'd made love to her the very next morning, before they were properly awake. Her soft, questing hands and receptive scent had got to him the way she always did.

Trying to leave after that would have been the height of callousness. He couldn't bring himself to do it anyway. Every time he tried to set some boundaries between them, she did some small thing he found charming and disarming or revealed a hidden tidbit about herself that roused the protector in him. He kept wondering who would keep the vagaries of life from knocking her around if he wasn't there to shield her?

He was becoming dependent on her in his own way, which was equally concerning. He liked her. She made him laugh and made him feel strong and necessary and powerful. She made him think and believe he was a better man than he was.

His palms were sweating as she walked down the aisle toward him, conscience heavy with the knowledge he was binding her to disgrace purely to feed this craving in him to have her by his side. Always.

The churn of cement in his gut didn't stop until they were pronounced husband and wife. Even then, he had to wonder how long it would take such a brilliant mind to realize she'd made a terrible mistake.

CHAPTER TEN

GIVEN THEIR RUSHED SCHEDULE, they had held their wedding midweek, the day before Pia's twelve-week scan. Her specialist appointment was the last thing on her calendar before she had two solid weeks of nothing to do, but she would have given up a kidney to stay in bed this morning.

"I should have canceled it," Angelo said when she yawned again, shivering with the force of it. "Or moved it to a later time."

"No." She fought another yawn. "Let's get this done and start our honeymoon. I'm looking forward to it."

He left a beat of silence for her to hear her own words. "Again, I wanted to stay in bed."

Now she was blushing, but she was pleased he was the teasing lover she saw so rarely these days. The car pulled into the underground entrance to the clinic and the interior of the car went into shadow. Seconds later Angelo slid out. He reached to help her, all humor gone from his expression as they hurried inside, hoping not to be spotted.

Speculation was rife that this was the reason for their rushed wedding, so she wasn't sure why they bothered. Twenty minutes later, they were reassured everything was fine. They could make their announcement and end all this secrecy.

She barely heard, too awestruck by the grayscale image with the fluttering heartbeat. She felt her hand grasped and squeezed. She dragged her gaze away and saw Angelo's eyes were damp as he fixated on the screen.

He met her gaze and his expression turned indescribably tender. He used his knuckle to brush away a tear on her cheek that she hadn't realized had brimmed and spilled over.

"I don't know why I'm so overcome," she said with a crooked smile. "It's biology. This is how reproduction happens."

"You're making us a little miracle." He caressed her jaw and looked back at the screen.

She looked back as well, hoping he was right.

* * *

Angelo rarely took vacations and knew this one would be a memory he would recall as one of the best times in his life. In fact, he was hoarding as many small moments as he could, making a point of enjoying the simplicity of his wife feeling for a dry bathing suit, failing to find one and seeking a new one from a drawer. She wore only a sarong, hair loose so she was an exotic island maiden. They were castaways in paradise and he never wanted to be rescued.

She stepped her bare feet into black bikini bottoms, pulled them up then loosened and dropped her sarong. She closed a strapless, neon pink top across her breasts, ran a finger around the edges, gave a jiggle and a wiggle and moved to the mirror. Frowned.

"I'm gaining weight!"

If she had gained a full kilo since telling him she was pregnant, he would be shocked, but there was a lovely ripeness to her figure that made his palms itch. The tug in the flesh between his thighs shouldn't have happened. They'd been in that bed only minutes ago.

This entire vacation was nothing but combing beaches, snorkeling and making love. Lather, rinse, repeat. Quite literally, he thought with a private smirk, thinking of the shower they'd taken before their most recent nap.

"I believe you're supposed to gain weight." He went across to stand behind her, hands finding the waist that might be a fraction thicker, but the changes were happening so gradually, he couldn't see it. He kissed her shoulder. "You're beautiful."

She turned in profile, eyed her abdomen. "The baby won't care if I'm fat."

He bit back agreeing or mentioning that he wouldn't, either. Only a very stupid man offered an opinion on weight.

"I want to hold our baby," she murmured, settling a hand beneath her navel. "It's what I'm looking forward to the most. The comfort and affection of holding someone."

"Hello?" he teased, pulling her arms around him before wrapping his arms around her.

She made a face as she came into contact with the damp bathing suit he hadn't been afraid to pull on. "You know what I mean."

"I don't. Explain it."

"My parents weren't demonstrative. I've always felt… I don't know. Lonesome, I guess. Needing affection."

"Even now?"

"Maybe not *right* now," she murmured, leaning against him, cheek nestling into his shoulder. "I wish we could stay here forever. Everything will change in a few days."

He couldn't refute that. He had the same sense of being in a bubble with thinning walls. It couldn't sustain this height of positive pressure and would burst any second.

His hands moved on her, trying to hold as much of her as possible against him. It was desire, the passion that always gripped him when he touched her, but it was more. He wanted to seal this connection they'd found, clamp it so tightly it became a part of him and could never be torn apart.

The need put urgency into the kiss he dropped on her mouth, but something else twined through him. A determination to hold on to what they had. Play it out. Make it last.

So even though the luscious sound in her

throat told him she was instantly receptive and eager, he gentled the stroke of his hands. She ran her open mouth up his neck and caught hungrily at him, and even though he was hard and ready and so desperate to be joined with her he might have begged if she commanded it, he took his time. He cupped her face and slowed their kiss and let it deepen until she was trembling against him.

He pressed soft kisses to soft skin, soothed her with long plays of his hands across her bare skin, giving both of them ample opportunity to enjoy the sizzle, allowing anticipation to build to a screaming pitch before he found the next plane of silken skin to worship.

He melted his beautiful ice princess inch by inch, waiting until her arms were heavy around his neck, her knees weak, before he eased her onto the mattress and stripped their minuscule bits of clothing.

Then he joined her. Kissed her. Cruised his mouth everywhere, tasting strawberry nipples and vanilla skin and the honey between her thighs. Her fist gripped his hair and her knee curled up and, because giving her pleasure gave him so much pleasure, he lazily swept her over the cliff into the smashing waves of orgasm.

Her cries of release sent the demons of desire into a frenzy within him, but he lashed them down, forced himself to patience, not allowing himself to rise over and thrust into her no matter how damp he was with perspiration or how badly he shook with craving.

He pressed kisses against her thighs and her calves and rolled her onto her stomach so he could lick the indent of her spine and pool his breath between her shoulder blades.

She shivered and squirmed and gasped, "What are you doing to me?"

"I'm making love to you." He wasn't sure if he said it or thought it, but it was all that was in his head. Sexual desire, but also a yearning to caress and please, explore and taste. Possess and give.

He combed his fingers into her hair, lifting it away from her neck so he could suck delicately against her nape. He bit lightly against her dampened skin so gooseflesh peppered her and she shuddered and groaned and lifted her hips with invitation.

He caressed her with his whole body, loving the feel of her beneath him like this. His erection nestled in the crease of her buttocks. Her thighs parted at his lightest touch, allowing him to stray his touch into her damp center where she called to him so inexorably.

Her movements beneath him drove him mad and still he only gathered her beneath him, stilling her so he could keep her right here. His. Forever.

"I want to touch you," she pleaded.

He drew back and she rolled into his arms, making him shake with relief and desire as her breasts, soft and supple, were crushed against his chest. Her nipples were hard points, her thigh downy as she stroked it against his hip. Her scent was all over him, clouding like an aphrodisiac, leaving him drugged and high.

"I love touching you like this," she confessed, hands roaming across the naked planes of his chest and hips, his thighs and buttocks and then—her confidence in bed had come a long way—to cup between his thighs. She purred as she weighed and shaped him, making him grit his teeth to hold on to his control.

As she guided him to the place he most wanted to be, he almost mourned the foreplay, wanting more time to claim every glorious cell of her body, but he was taken over by the animal that needed its mate. He settled atop her and sank into her with a ragged groan. The world opened before him. Pia was his world. All of her was his.

And this, the slow pump of his hips, stoking more pleasure than any man had a right to, was everything he ever needed.

As Pia's heart rate slowed, she reminded herself that climax released a host of chemicals in the brain. This sense of security and eye-dampening closeness was as biologically normal as her sensitive nipples and weight gain.

Love also caused those same symptoms. Or so she'd heard.

Was that what this was? This emotional dependence and sensation that she would split in half from the joy wanting to burst from within her, just because his weight pinned her and his skin was still damp with perspiration?

She was beginning to fear it was, and she didn't know what to do about it. Tell him? What if he didn't care? What if he didn't return her feelings?

Her haze of satisfaction and rumination was broken by his ringtone.

"I told you we had to get out of here before that happened." His sexy rasp tickled her ear.

"Mmm… My fault for falling under you."

His smile flashed as his heavy arm left off caressing her shoulder and the blanketing warmth of him rolled away.

Definitely love, she thought, as that brief smile struck like sunshine in her heart.

He was maintaining a light work schedule, all but a few key ringtones set to ignore.

"Killian," he said as he frowned at the screen. "I have to take it."

Roman Killian was the husband of their engagement photographer, Melodie, but he also owned and ran the global company that provided all of Angelo's security needs.

Pia heard Killian's voice as clearly as Angelo's.

"Arson," Killian stated bluntly. "Brazen and designed for maximum damage. All the staff had gone to their own homes so there are no injuries. They have the suspect. Darius Gomez. He claims to be your brother."

Pia sat up with alarm, fingers searching for the edge of a sheet as she scanned to the glass doors leading onto the private beach of their luxury villa.

"Keep it as quiet as you can, but prosecute to the full extent of the law," Angelo ordered. "Not an ounce of leniency. Add whatever security my staff requires to feel safe while they clean up."

Any lingering warmth from their lovemaking was gone. His tone was hard and sharp as jagged glass, shearing off her buzz of gratification.

"Now we find out," he said gruffly as he ended the call and tossed his phone onto the mattress between them as though throwing down a gauntlet.

"Find out what?"

"How you'll react. I'll release my side ahead of any lies they try to concoct." Her lover was gone and here was the brute who gave no quarter to those who had wronged him. Who stared unwaveringly into her eyes and dared her to try to talk him out of the action he intended to take.

Her heart stuttered in her chest and she tried to swallow, but her throat was too dry. She wanted to stop him to spare him whatever suffering was coming, but stopping him was futile, she could tell. The only other thing she could do was wall up her own emotions to allow room for his.

She nodded jerkily. "I'll call Rico. He needs to know first."

They went straight back to Spain, rather than going to California.

Pia had a very difficult conversation with her brother while Angelo was barking orders into his own phone.

"You should have told me the minute you knew he'd been here uninvited. Do you know how they behaved toward Poppy?" Rico had never spoken to her so harshly.

"Angelo is not one of them." She would *not* allow that comparison. Ever. "Look," she tried in a more conciliatory tone. "I understand why you're angry, but it wasn't my story to tell."

"Now it is? When everything is going to hell in a handcart? He didn't even have the mettle to tell me himself?"

"I wanted to do it—"

Rico hung up on her before she could explain.

She didn't mention Rico's reaction to Angelo. He was moving beyond damage control into aggressor. His press release dropped while they were in the air and he had a news conference scheduled immediately after they landed. He not only didn't ask her to stand at his side for it, he sent her to her mother's.

"I want to be with you," she argued.

"No, you don't."

She caught her breath, hearing it as an accusation until he added, "I want to know you're insulated from any further acts of aggression.

Darius is in custody, but that doesn't mean Tomas won't try something."

Now she would be worried sick about him, standing at a podium like a target, but he was in crisis mode. She didn't add to his concerns by arguing. She did what she had always done when there were bigger problems to solve. She stepped out of the way.

Going to her parents' house was no picnic. Her father was in Madrid, which made little difference aside from the fact her mother commented, "I suppose he'll have to hold a press conference of his own."

Pia felt rather helpless. "Angelo didn't mean for this to happen, Mother."

"Didn't he?" La Reina asked with a blithe look. "He seems to have been seeking blood this whole time. Why on earth did he insist on that pageant of a wedding otherwise?"

Pia never talked back to her mother, not in an outburst of emotion, but she cried, "That was for our baby! You were on board with a big wedding, too."

"Pia." Her mother's tone dripped with condescension. "That was not the wedding I envisioned for you. This is not the marriage. Especially now."

"Well, he's the husband I wanted," she spat back, shaking at the confrontation while her mother only gave her a faint frown.

"Are you able to take hold of your emotions and discuss damage control?" La Reina stirred cream into her tea, the clatter of her spoon jangling Pia's nerves.

The man she loved, really, truly, deeply loved, was going through hell. Pia wanted to cry and rage and throw a tantrum, she was so upset for him, but the one thing her mother had taught her was to shove aside that sort of reaction and think logically about what could be done on a practical level.

Dragging in a deep breath, she found her composure and firmly pressed it over her shredded control. "Of course," she insisted.

"Do you have any influence over him at all?"

She almost lost it again, but managed to hang on to a civil tone. "He is entitled to his outrage, Mother. Were you aware of what his mother was going through when it happened?"

"I barely knew them," she dismissed. "There

was a rumor the stepdaughter had been with the gardener's son and that's why she wasn't out in society. Until this press release, I believed the news reports that she had died after a brief illness."

"Doesn't it sicken you that the truth has been covered up? Or are you only upset that we've been attached to it?"

"Why *are* we attached to it, Pia? You've never been promiscuous. Have you heard any of the statements he's made? He loathes what we represent. He is not Poppy or Sorcha, coming into our lives through honest fallibility and with an earnest desire to be one of us. He targeted you. All of this has been orchestrated for maximum damage to more than his brothers. He's trying to take down the aristocracy."

"That's not true." She didn't explain that Angelo hadn't known who she was that first night. Her family still thought they'd been dating in private before the masquerade ball. "His mother was treated horribly," Pia continued fervently. "If he married me to champion her, I can live with that." Mostly. Of course she wanted her marriage to be more than that, but at least it was an altruistic motive, not the calculating one her mother was suggesting.

"You continue to possess an unfortunate streak of compassion." Her mother sighed. "If he wanted help with his battle over his mother, he should have gone about it differently, not seduced you into his scandal. He manipulated you into helping him achieve influence. Now he's swinging a scythe with the Montero name on it."

She shook her head, but her mother was sowing a seed of doubt.

"This isn't justice he's seeking, it's vengeance," her mother continued. "You understand he's been buying up his brothers' debts? Placing liens on their properties? Buying stocks in a hostile takeover to force them out? His aim is to ruin them, Pia."

"So?" Maybe it was a vigilante move, but she didn't blame him for his ruthless tactics.

"You're too smart to allow yourself to be used."

Pia wished she could claim Angelo had married her because he loved her, not that her mother would see any value in such a declaration, but Pia would. No such words had passed their lips, however. And now, all kinds of doubts were prickling to life inside her.

"Do you insist on staying married to him?" her mother asked stiffly.

"Yes." She wished her voice had come out stronger.

Her mother's mouth pinched. "Very well. Let's find our best path forward."

Utterly drained, Pia was trying to recover with the cool weight of a lavender eye pillow across her brow. A chamomile tea steeped on the table beside her, but she'd chosen to rest in the front parlor so she would greet Angelo the moment he turned up.

She was snapped out of her doze by the chirp of brakes. Raised voices caused a commotion in the courtyard. It sounded like Angelo and Rico.

She stood up too quickly and had to grasp at the back of the sofa to catch her balance as her head swam. As soon as she was steady, she hurried out the front doors.

Angelo had arrived in a car she didn't recognize, and Rico had parked behind him on the circular drive. They were standing between the bumpers, car doors open, locked in a heated exchange.

"It's my *house*," Rico spat. "My wife spent the last year turning it into a *home*. How dare you jeopardize that?"

"Rico!" Pia trotted down the steps, afraid they would come to blows. "What's wrong? What happened?" She inserted herself between them.

"His brothers are trying to renege on their sale of the estate," Rico barked. "Because he's making a claim on their proceeds from it. And because *he* stole property they left there. Thanks to *you*," Rico added in a sideswipe at her.

"I took what belonged to my mother. Her share of the family fortune, bequeathed to me." Angelo took Pia's shoulders to set her aside as he tried to step forward into combat.

Pia slapped her hand onto his chest, keeping him from advancing, but the ire in him nearly bowled her over.

"Make them a settlement for it. Make this

go away," Rico demanded, gaze locked with Angelo's.

"I don't want it to go away. I want them to rot in hell. If you don't think they should, you can rot there with them."

"At the expense of my wife and children?" Rico was outraged.

"Angelo, please," Pia begged, as caught between them emotionally as she was physically. "Please calm down and let's discuss this rationally."

"Oh, there's a surprise, coming from you." He brushed her off him, taking a step back so the verbal and physical rejection was equally devastating. "Let's be rational then," he said to Rico with scathing sarcasm. "You bought that estate at a bargain price in a backroom deal. *You* pay the settlement they want."

"Angelo."

She was genuinely shocked and appalled at the vindictiveness spewing out of him. Distantly she understood that he must have been through a lot today, but her mother's comments seemed to hold more water as she saw how much thirst for punishment was in him.

"That's not fair. Listen, I'm not saying your brothers are innocent, but don't confuse their crimes with your father's. Should they be held to account for his actions? Do you want our child judged on the way you're behaving? That means you have to pay for your father's crimes, too. Don't be like them," she pleaded. "Stop this cycle of hatred."

"Why? Because it's inconvenient for *you*? So you can go on living in your damned ivory tower, ignoring what my mother went through? You're all the damned same! Of all the women on all the rooftops, I had to get the one who thinks preserving this—" he flung a hand toward the villa "—is more important than common decency."

"Who the hell are you to talk about decency after the way you targeted her to pursue a vendetta?" Rico demanded.

Angelo choked out a humorless laugh, his gaze careening into her own.

As their gazes caught and clashed, his stare hardened. He seemed to search into her soul, seeing all the insecurities and doubts her mother had planted inside her. Now Rico was making the same accusation and Pia knew she shouldn't give those charges any weight, but she was looking for reassurance in Angelo's expression and seeing only a flinch of angry contempt.

And a flash of hurt that was so profound it speared her like a paralyzing poisoned dart.

"Angelo." Her lips were numb as she moved jerkily forward to set a hand on his arm.

He pulled away, his profile cast in iron.

"Angelo, I love you," she whispered, voice faint because she had never said the words before. Her throat was nothing but sandpaper, her chest a broken shell. She didn't know how to offer her heart when it was such a tender, thin-skinned little thing. It was new and delicate as butterfly wings, beating in her cupped hands.

"Don't." His head went back in recoil. "Even if it were true, how long would it last?"

Even if it were true? His rejection of her feelings was so shockingly *typical*, it knocked the breath clean out of her.

"I'm never going to be one of you. I don't *want* to be."

"I'm not one of them, either. You know I'm

not," she choked, stricken that he would lump her in with those horrid people who'd failed to ask questions and had turned a blind eye, leaving his mother to her suffering.

"No, you're special, Pia. You are. Far better than I deserve." His gaze came back, resolute. "You know it. Your family knows it. *I've* always known my illegitimate hands shouldn't be handling the fine china. You deserve better than me, Pia. You genuinely do." His voice became agonizingly gentle even as he dismissed every tender moment that had bound them together. "I can't bring you down with me. It's only going to get worse. Turns out money does not buy respectability." His eyes were shadowed with futility. "Best to end it here and now, before I do any more damage."

When he turned away, she lifted a hand, feet rooted with shock. She didn't realize he was getting into the car and leaving until the engine started and he pulled away.

Then her breastbone fractured and her throat strangled on a tormented, "*No*—" but he was already shooting through the gate and gone.

"He's right. You're better off without him,"

Rico said, grasping her arm, trying to hug her. "We'll look after you. And the baby."

Ice formed around her, stiffening her joints, making her brother's attempt to comfort her an awkward, unwelcome embrace. She wanted Angelo to hold her and look after her and their baby. She couldn't breathe. She had laid herself bare to the man she loved and he'd left.

No one would ever love her. *Ever.*

"I'll take you inside," Rico said.

"No." Pia withdrew into her protective casing the way one of her beloved hermit crabs cringed back into its borrowed shell. She would need a bigger one to hold this amount of heartbreak. She didn't know how she would carry the weight of it, but that was another day's job.

"Go home to Poppy," she managed to say. "She'll be worried. I'll sell my house to pay your legal bills. You won't lose your home."

"Don't be ridiculous."

"It makes perfect sense," she said with one of her well-practiced expressions of cool reason. The profound loneliness washing over her was as familiar as returning to a big, empty house. "This was my error in judgment. Let me make amends."

CHAPTER ELEVEN

From the moment Angelo had been forced to release his mother's story, he'd been in agony. All his helpless, furious guilt at being unable to help her, or prevent her early death, had risen up to turn him on a spit of fire.

He hadn't wanted Pia anywhere near the ugliness of his news conference. The fresh accusations and blatant lies Tomas had told, trying to absolve Darius from his crime along with their father, had made him sick.

And ashamed. He was so damned ashamed to have one single drop of their blood in him. Even more chagrined that he wanted his wife by his side while he was standing knee-deep in family closet filth.

He'd had the strength to insulate her from the brunt of negative attention they'd been forced to endure, but after weathering that first blast, he had wanted only one thing. To get back to Pia. To crawl into the bubble of calm she always provided—not that he believed all his problems would disappear, but they would be bearable, he'd thought, if he could only hold her.

Rico had caught up to him in the courtyard before he'd even climbed from his car. Of course Tomas was going after the house, claiming some sort of conspiracy between them to defraud him of the jewelry. Angelo's brothers were grasping at any straw within reach.

Angelo hadn't been at his rational best. Nothing in him had wanted to give an inch to anyone. When Pia had tried to reason with him, he hadn't been able to see through his haze. What he had glimpsed, however, had been a harrowing doubt in her eyes. Justified qualms over why he had married her.

Her lack of faith in him had nearly cut him in half, but what did he expect? That she would take the side of someone his brothers were calling an "abomination"?

When she had then claimed to love him, he

hadn't been able to take it in. Hadn't been able to accept it, given the ugliness he had brought into her life by forcing their marriage. There *had* been a part of him that had seized the chance to marry her because of her name. He *had* wanted vengeance above anything else.

He didn't deserve to be loved for any of that.

Stop the cycle of hatred, she had said, and he had realized how twisted he had become. If he kept it up, he would be no better than the darkness he had come from.

Angelo reached the airfield in a daze, feeling as though he was bleeding out and had to do something, anything, to stanch the flow. He called his lawyer as he climbed aboard his jet.

"Tell Tomas to stop going after Rico's house. I'll put the proceeds from the sale of the jewelry into a trust until ownership is established." Tomas would accept the deal since his attempt to rewrite the estate sale would be expensive and he had even less chance of winning that than he did in proving the jewelry was his.

"The *señora* isn't traveling with us?" the attendant asked.

"No." He was going back to view the damage at the house. "Double," he ordered as his customary scotch was poured.

He brooded and drank until he landed. Then he walked through a house with a corner blown out where he and Pia had sat for their engagement photo. Plastic sheets hung over the space. The open plan interior had been stripped down to subfloor and studs, but there were still scorch marks on the ceiling.

The rest of the house was intact. Angelo went up to the room where Pia had joined him for only a few short days, but the whole villa felt imbued with her presence. He instantly knew he wouldn't be able to sleep in that bed without her. Wouldn't be able to live here without thinking of her every minute of every day.

He would think of her regardless, no matter where he ended up.

How was he going to live without her? Without their baby?

He nearly went to his knees as he realized what he had done. Pushing her away had been the right thing to do, though. Hadn't it?

Eyes wet, breath rattling in his chest, he left the room and was drawn into the next one, the nursery. Sea-green walls were decorated with shells and seahorses and tropical fish. The crib was assembled with a mobile of starfish dangling over one end.

All of this had been chosen by Pia. He had watched her browse and light up with quiet glee as she found the different items and sent links to their decorator.

She loved their baby—he knew she did—yet he hadn't believed her when she had spoken the words to him. He'd still been seeing the stark guilt in her expression when her brother had hurled his accusations. Angelo knew what they all thought of him. He had been reeling and devastated that his wife believed any of it.

How could she love him *and* doubt him?

What did he expect, though? He hadn't been completely honest with her. He hadn't admitted to his own love, even though it was such a force in him he was pulsing in agony at being apart from her.

He hadn't allowed himself to say it or acknowledge it or even fully feel it because, deep down, he'd been convinced he wasn't good enough for her. He had been biding his time until she realized it and rejected him. He had *expected* to lose her.

She had promised that if his truth came to light, it wouldn't change her commitment to him or their marriage, but he hadn't given her a chance to prove that she would stand by him. In fact, he'd sent her to her mother's, then thrown her declaration of love back in her face. And left her. Like a fool.

"Pia," he groaned with anguish.

He couldn't stay here. There was a giant hole in the side of his house and a bigger one in his heart.

Two days later, Angelo sought out Rico at the Montero corporate headquarters.

He had told Pia once that he was willing to risk all that he had for something he wanted badly enough. That included his pride, but his wife and child were worth it.

He was shown into Cesar's office, where both brothers stood in solidarity, Cesar behind the massive mahogany desk, Rico beside it.

Angelo eschewed handshakes and the empty chair in favor of stating his business.

"Tomas and Darius have been neutralized. Not like that," he added with swift, arid sarcasm when two pairs of brows shot up. "In exchange for them signing a binding promise not to talk to the press, I have agreed to let them keep what they have left. If they step out of line, I will finish them and make no apologies for it. You caught me on a bad day," he said to Rico. "I am capable of rational behavior."

"Tell your wife. She wants to sell her house to finance my legal bill."

"That's ridiculous. No," Angelo dismissed the idea. "Invoice me for any inconveniences you've suffered."

"I will," Cesar said bluntly. "Including the prenup negotiations and the wedding. You could have saved us a lot of time, money and trouble."

Cesar's words were a kick to the chest, but Angelo managed to stay on his feet. "We're staying married."

"You're not taking another round out of her. Do you understand how sensitive she is?" Cesar set his knuckles on his desk. "How cruel it was to target her like that?"

"I didn't target her! I didn't know who she wa—" He cut himself off, angry with himself for saying too much, but Rico swore in comprehension.

"When you made that remark about the rooftop the other day, I didn't want to believe it. Are you telling me you two only met that night? That you—"

"I am not discussing our private life with you," Angelo said firmly, pointing a finger in warning. He personally didn't care one iota. His sense of modesty was very low. Pia, however? "Do *you* understand how sensitive your sister is? How *shy*? How *smart*? Don't stand here and act concerned about her when she's out there earning doctorates two years before you did and you can't even be bothered to show up and give her a round of applause."

Rico lost some of his bluster. He sent a disgruntled look toward Cesar.

"Poppy wanted to organize something. Lily got sick and it slipped our mind."

"Sorcha called Mother to set up a lunch. You'd think she pitched overthrowing the government." Cesar straightened off his desk and

262 BOUND BY THEIR NINE-MONTH SCANDAL

sighed. He folded his arms as he regarded Angelo. "I'm smart enough to know how smart my sister is, yes. I've asked her to join our research team several times. She's always preferred fieldwork and biology, but I hoped once the baby was born, she might finally consider my offer more seriously."

"*Did* you get her pregnant on purpose?" Rico demanded.

"Wow." Angelo tilted him an affronted glare. "Delightful as Pia's family has turned out to be, *no*, I didn't resort to time-tested methods to become a member. You could bowl tenpins with those balls, asking a question like that when you didn't plan *your* family."

Rico narrowed his eyes while Cesar deadpanned, "I've seen them. Five pins, tops."

Madre de Dios.

"I married Pia because we're expecting a baby. Because I want to be a better father than I had." Angelo had briefly lost sight of that, but never would again. "I'm staying married to her because I'm in love with her. That means, for her sake, we're going to learn to play nice." He drew a small circle in the air. "I thought cleaning up my mess with my brothers was a good start. Now, you have a pleasant evening, gentlemen. Convey my regards to your infinitely more charming wives."

"Same," Rico shot at his back.

Angelo had texted Pia while he was on the island, telling her the security team had deemed it safe to move back into her home. He checked there first, but the housekeeper said she had packed a bag and left instructions to ready the house for sale.

Angelo reversed that order and presumed Pia had decided to stay at her mother's.

He went there and was informed that Pia had left two days ago for her own house. When he expressed his dissatisfaction with that information, he was forced to wait twenty minutes before La Reina deigned to see him.

He gave her the report he'd given her sons. "Aside from lingering speculation in the press, which should die off fairly quickly, this should all be over."

"Thank you for informing me." With a smile of pressed civility, she rose.

"Your staff tells me Pia isn't here," he said,

preventing her from leaving. "She's not in her home and not answering my texts."

"That's to be expected."

"What do you mean?" Angelo bristled, suspecting she was deliberately punishing him, but he couldn't read anything malicious in her expression. No enjoyment of his frustration, only a vague puzzlement with his continued presence.

"I mean that she does this. She travels out of range, thereby taking a few days to respond to messages. It's something you should expect of her as common behavior."

"So you don't know where she went? Aren't you concerned?"

"She's a grown adult. She makes her own schedule."

"She's pregnant."

"She's not foolish." Her mouth twitched slightly as if she heard the irony in her own words, given her daughter's choice in husband. "Do you have reason to believe there would be a medical issue?"

"No, but…" Angelo clenched his teeth, wondering how Pia had withstood a lifetime of this stonewalling. "Did she—" He could barely bring himself to ask. "Is she avoiding me? Seeking a legal separation?"

La Reina frowned. "I should think you'd be the first to know that, not me."

"So she didn't say anything like that to you?"

La Reina rang for her assistant and asked with exaggerated patience, "Do we know where my daughter is?"

Clearly "we" didn't.

"A research trip, *señora,*" was the unhelpful answer.

"There you are. She'll turn up when she's finished her fieldwork," La Reina said.

"Where did she go? When is she coming back?" Angelo asked the assistant.

"I'm sorry. I don't have that information, *señor.* She books her own travel."

Frustrated, he returned to her home and went into her office to see if he could figure out where she'd gone. Why had she left without telling anyone where she was going? It didn't portend well and left a sick knot in his gut.

It made him think she really was fine with

ending their marriage so she could go back to the life she'd led before.

He had a quick peek at her social media profiles, half thinking he would approach some of the people he'd met during their goodwill tour before their wedding. He quickly realized none of them were on there. Her friend list consisted of her immediate family and her privacy settings were locked down. Her only public content was the photographs he'd once thought proved she lived a globe-trotting life in exotic locations.

Now he knew her better, which cast a fresh light on the remoteness in her snapshots. While they'd been in Australia, he'd taken several photos of her, and she'd said, "I'm usually alone and I hate taking selfies so I'm never in my photos."

Until this moment, he hadn't heard the deep loneliness in that statement. Now he saw it clearly in the beautiful places she visited without having anyone with her to share her experience.

He looked more closely at her home office. Every wall was covered in bookshelves. Three of the nonfiction titles were written by her—where the hell had those come from? Why had she never mentioned that she understood economics well enough to write investment strategies for non-professionals?

There were dozens of textbooks on a range of subjects, a handful of self-help tomes on public speaking and networking, two shelves of dog-eared romance novels and a shelf stuffed to the gills with journals. They were all neatly labeled with dates.

He took one out at random and saw nothing but numbers and dates and Latin names. So much information gathered and filtered through that sharp brain of hers, distilled and shared on her terms.

Because she found human interactions so difficult? Or because she had no one with whom to share her discoveries?

His heart truly began to ache, then. She had admitted to feeling lonely most of her life. He'd seen how she struggled to connect. All this time, he'd feared that she would never feel anything genuine toward him when maybe all he'd had to do was let her know how much she meant to him. How much he loved her.

He loved her and missed her and not knowing where she'd gone was torture.

But finding her turned out to be as simple as checking their joint credit card statement. The Faroe Islands. Where the hell was that?

He called his pilot and was soon headed in the direction of Iceland.

Over a lifetime of nursing loneliness and scorn, Pia had discovered there was a strangely comforting symmetry in being physically miserable when she was emotionally miserable.

There was also something reassuring in returning to familiar routines. She set her trusty, well-worn, gel cushion on a suitable rock, propped her journal on her crooked knee while balancing an umbrella with the same hand and used her free hand to begin making notes on the colony of seals below her.

The wind blew the rain into her face and onto her page, but that was why she wore a rubber coat and used pencil instead of ink. The damp sank into her bones, but she had brought a cushion and a thermos of hot tea as consolation. The man she loved would never love her, but that was why she was here. Even forsaken souls could be useful to humanity if they didn't mind a little tedium and isolation.

The bark of the seals and rush of the waves drowned out the sound of footsteps until the boots appeared in her peripheral vision.

She gasped and looked up, telling herself it was a local who had tramped out to ask her what she was doing, but she already knew it was Angelo. Her body knew it before her eyes confirmed it.

He scanned the small harbor below, but looked at her as she tilted the umbrella back so she could see him. His brows pulled into a frown.

"What are you doing?"

"Working."

"I thought you wanted to set up a pregnancy study?"

She glanced down, almost saying that what she studied only mattered to her and she was beginning to think she didn't matter to anyone.

She slanted the umbrella over herself again.

"I told you I like to collect data when I need to think."

"You could have told me where you were going."

"You didn't tell me where *you* were going."

"Touché." Beside her, she saw his hand give a restive flex. "I went to the island. The house is a mess, but the nursery looks good. It should all be repaired and ready for us by the time the baby arrives."

"Us?" She bobbled the umbrella and her nerveless fingers nearly shot the pencil across the pebbly ground. "You and the baby?"

"All of us."

"You ended our marriage, Angelo. You *left*." Her chest locked up and she could only blindly stare at the chop of white beards on the gray scroll of waves. She had come away because she couldn't face that he'd abandoned her so unceremoniously.

"You said you wouldn't let my past change your commitment to our marriage."

"It didn't."

His hand caught the fabric of her umbrella and shoved it back so he could see her. Rain had soaked into his hair and was running down his face. The spitting drops peppered her face as she looked up at him.

"Then why are you here?" he growled.

"You said we were over. I needed to feel like myself again. To do something I know how to do well instead of…" *Faking it. Banging into walls. Falling in love and failing at marriage.*

"I was worried about you."

"The baby is fine. I spoke to the doctor before I came away. She said it was okay to come."

"I was worried about *you*."

"No one ever worries about me." She tried to shove her umbrella back into place.

He didn't let her. "*I* worry about you."

"The baby—"

"*You*," he nearly shouted.

She was so startled, she let go of the handle. He lost his own grip and the umbrella tumbled away in the wind.

Pia didn't move, only tugged her woolen hat more firmly onto her head.

"I'm still one of the blue bloods you love to hate," she reminded him.

"You're the only blue blood I can stand," he muttered. "My own included. Hopefully our baby will have more of yours than mine."

"You'll love it either way?"

"I will." His tortured gaze shifted to the water. "I can't change what I am, Pia. Sometimes I hate myself for existing. For causing so much pain to someone I loved."

"I can't speak for her, Angelo, but it sounds like she loved you exactly as you were, despite the blood you carry. That blood doesn't change how I feel about you or how I'll feel about our baby."

"How do you feel about me?"

Her eyes welled. She looked down at the page that was growing soaked.

"Do you want to hear how I feel? Angry," he said, sounding incensed. "I'm angry on your behalf. I hate that your father doesn't see how special you are and that your mother values her wealth and standing over the suffering she causes you."

"It doesn't—"

"Don't say it doesn't matter. It matters. *You* matter, Pia. You matter to me. But I understand that she won't change. Neither of them will. I didn't mean to make you cry."

She dug up a tissue and he crouched to catch her eyes with his own.

"Your turn. Tell me how you feel," he commanded.

"Grateful." It was a cowardly admission. A small, easy one because she didn't have the courage to make a bigger one. It was true, though. "No matter what happens between us, I will always be grateful you gave me someone who will love me as I am."

His expression altered. Torment seemed to grip him. "Pia, I'm that person. *I* love you exactly as you are."

Her heart lurched and she felt so dizzy, she nearly fell off the rock. "You can't."

"Of course I can. That's why I left. I couldn't stand that I was doing it again, hurting someone I loved. It was terrible logic because I wound up hurting you anyway. I'm looking forward to you preventing me from being so stupid again."

"But I'm not…lovable."

"Of course you are. You're funny and smart and kind and sensitive. Sexy as *hell*. Brave."

"See, you're lying."

"Modest. Very beautiful, although I know you don't care about that. Curious and warm."

"Robotic."

"Introspective. Affectionate." He touched her knee where her jeans were soaked through.

She was starting to shiver, but not from the cold. She couldn't hold her mouth steady. "Why are you saying all this?" He was inspiring such a depth of hope, but she was so afraid to believe.

"Because I love you." His expression became very grave while her heart teetered and rolled. "I could not have gone through this without you, Pia. I couldn't have faced my past and moved beyond it. I would have let it destroy me if I hadn't been falling in love with you this whole time. I wouldn't be capable of love if you weren't here, inspiring it in me."

"I don't know what to say to that."

"Tell me you love me. Please." His used the backs of his fingers to gather the raindrops dripping off her jaw. He swiped his hand on his wet jeans. "I promise you I will believe you this time."

"That word doesn't seem like enough for the way I feel. It doesn't seem like it matches all those wonderful things you just said. You're—"

He cupped her jaw with his damp palm and his wet thumb silenced her lips.

"You don't care about my past. That's all that matters to me."

Her chin crinkled under the line of his thumb while her insides were nothing but trapped birds flittering every which way.

"It can't be this easy after it was so h-hard." Her throat was tight, her voice a mere squeak. "For so l-long."

"It won't always be easy, *mi amor*," he said with tender understanding. "Sometimes I will tell you to come in out of the rain and you'll make me stand here and count chickens with you. Other times I'll punish you by making you dress up in designer gowns and talk to strangers."

"And you'll still love me despite my petulant sighs?"

"I will love you *because* of them. Because they will remind me you're there for my sake, not for designer gowns. It's inevitable that we argue over the small nonsense of life, but it won't compare to the harmony I feel waking next to you or holding your hand in mine."

He took hers now, made a tiny adjustment to her rings. Brought her hand to his lips and kissed her trembling fingers.

"I want to build a life with you, Pia. Not one that seeks vengeance. One that fosters love. I need you in my life, every day, helping me do that."

"I wanted this so badly and I've been trying so hard not to hope for it. It hurt so much when I was convinced it couldn't come true. Now I'm afraid I'm going to wake up and find out I really am dreaming."

He bit her knuckle hard enough to threaten pain.

"Ouch! Hey." She scowled, trying to snatch her hand away in reaction.

He grinned and kept her hand in his as he stood. He gave a gentle tug. "Can we get out of the rain?"

She glanced at her ruined notebook, pages curled and turning to pulp.

"I'll buy you a bowl of soup," he coaxed. "We can talk about a foundation to address the effects of climate change on marine mammals or…" He scanned the beach. "What are you doing here?"

"Do you really want to know?" She was embarrassed, but trusted him enough to know that when he laughed at her, it would be in the kindest way possible. "I named them several years ago. I check on them when I'm feeling blue. I like to see who is hooking up with whom and count the new babies."

His valiant struggle to keep a straight face was love in its purest form.

"I also have a colony of penguins and some polar bears I like to track." She rubbed her nose where rain was dripping and causing a tickle. "A pod of whales. Way too many dolphins, but they're so playful and cute."

"I'm excited to hear all about them," he assured her with a solemn nod. "Soup?"

She rose, gave a little shrug to knock the worst of the gathered rain off her coat.

"Or we could go to my hotel room," she suggested. "Warm up in the shower before we dry off and go to bed. Maybe not talk much at all for a while."

"Then order room service? See, this is why I love being married to a woman who is smarter than me." He helped her gather her things, then stood with her in the rain a moment longer. Long enough to kiss her senseless.

With his arm firm around her, he drew her from the empty beach into their shared future.

EPILOGUE

Eighteen months later...

"CAN WE HOLD JELLY?" Lily asked, one arm curled trustingly around her Tío Cesar's neck while he clasped her affectionately against his chest.

Angelo had a very difficult time denying his nieces and nephews anything, particularly sweet Lily with her high voice and innocently batted lashes and her hilarious shortening of Angelica's name to Jelly.

Tío Cesar was another story. Angelo enjoyed a good-natured trashy relationship with his wife's brothers, well developed over the year since they'd all had their litter of newborns and he'd partnered with them on an alloy for a gaming console they were jointly developing.

"You're shameless," he said to Cesar, nodding at Lily, who coaxed with a wave of her free arm, entreating her younger cousin to join them.

"I like to connect with my nieces. That's how one keeps the title Favorite Uncle. Pro tip," Cesar advised in a facetious drawl.

Fighting words. Angelo narrowed his eyes. "Wait until *your* daughter's birthday." He would spoil her enough for a lifetime.

"*Please*, Jelly?" Lily begged. "Tío Cesar wants to read us a book."

Angelica peeked from where she had her face buried in Angelo's neck. She wasn't particularly shy, but she made strange with her uncles sometimes, mostly because she didn't see them as often as she saw Poppy and Sorcha and the children.

She had also just woken from her nap to a lot of people and attention, not that they were making a big deal out of her first birthday. Pia had invited her brothers and their families to spend the weekend at their island home because it was the middle of the summer and they all enjoyed an excuse to spend time together. The grandparents had chosen not to make the journey for something so frivolous, which kept it to a laid-back gathering where the children could be as boisterous as they liked.

"Want to cuddle with Lily and Tío?" Angelo asked his daughter.

"Maybe Brenna will join us," Cesar said of his daughter, noting the little firecracker was working up to fight her brother, Mateo, to the death over a pool noodle.

"You on that, Rico?" Angelo mocked as Angelica went to Cesar and Rico waded into the dispute, his year-old son naked on his hip.

"Tío!" Enrique called from the diving board. "Watch me flip."

"Where are the women? How did we get outnumbered? Ah, Memo," Rico muttered as a wet stain appeared on his shirt. "I knew that would happen. Here." He handed his son to Angelo.

Angelo diapered his nephew while Rico caught Brenna back from chasing her brother down the stairs into deeper water. He plopped Brenna with her father and the girls, then threw off his stained shirt and cannonballed into the pool to soak the boys.

"I told you they'd have everything under control," Sorcha said as the women appeared with trays of food and drink. Memo went to Poppy, then pointed at his father in the pool so she took him across to hand him in to Rico.

"I'm insulted there was any doubt in us." Angelo scooped Pia close and stage-whispered, "Thank God you got here when you did."

She chuckled and looped her arms around his waist, gazing over the convivial chaos of their pool party. "This is nice."

"It is."

"Okay," Poppy said, coming back to uncork a bottle of wine. "I've been very excited for this day. Our first vintage and everyone is weaned, right? We girls finally get to split a bottle of wine?"

Pia wrinkled her nose and looked at Angelo. They had suspected they wouldn't be able to keep it under wraps a full three months.

"Really?" Poppy asked with shock, catching their look while bright tears came into her eyes.

"We didn't mean to," Pia admitted sheepishly. "It just happened."

"Oh, we know how it 'just happens,'" Sorcha teased.

"Too true," Poppy said, coming to hug both of them. "That's wonderful news. Congratulations."

Much later, when Angelo was lying replete next to his wife, her damp body relaxed against his, he said, "Do you remember our honeymoon?"

"I think we were just there," she said on a luxurious sigh and a slither of her naked skin against his own. She settled her head more comfortably on his shoulder.

He smiled into the dark. "That's what I meant. I remember thinking I had to memorize it because I might never be that happy again, but I am. Often."

"A wise person once told me that happiness is fleeting, not a state of being."

"He might not have been as smart as the woman he was talking to."

She brought her thigh up to rest across his

stomach. Her face turned into his skin as she kissed above his heart. "For the record, after much dedicated research, I have concluded that happiness is a goal worth pursuing."

"Hypothesis proven?"

"Beyond a shadow of a doubt."

* * * * *

LET'S TALK

Romance

For exclusive extracts, competitions
and special offers, find us online:

f facebook.com/millsandboon

○ @millsandboonuk

◆ @millsandboon

Or get in touch on 0844 844 1351*

For all the latest titles coming soon,
visit millsandboon.co.uk/nextmonth

*Calls cost 7p per minute plus your phone company's price per
minute access charge